TWO HEARTS IN WINTER

TWO HEARTS IN WINTER

OCEAN CITY BOARDWALK SERIES
BOOK 2

DONNA FASANO

Two Hearts in Winter

Paperback ISBN: 978-1-939000-32-3

eBook ISBN: 978-1-939000-33-0

Find the author:

Facebook – Facebook.com/DonnaFasanoAuthor

Twitter – Twitter.com/DonnaFaz

Pinterest – Pinterest.com/DonnaFaz

Instagram – Instagram.com/Donna_Fasano

Contents

Loss and betrayal have caused Heather Phillips to give up on love. She's thrown herself into running The Lonely Loon, her Bed and Breakfast located on the boardwalk of Ocean City, Maryland. The "off season" in this tourist town is usually a time of rest and reflection for her; however, DB Atwell, a famous author, arrives at The Loon for the winter to finish his long-overdue novel. Daniel, too, has faced grief, and tragedy continues to haunt him. Once Heather and Daniel meet, their lives will never be the same.

Reminiscent of Nights in Rodanthe by Nicholas Sparks and culminating in a happily-ever-after similar to the great Nora Roberts, Two Hearts in Winter is a story about learning to let go of the past, about realizing that, though hardship affects us, it need not define us, *and about coming to understand and truly believe that beauty is sometimes covered in scars. The human heart has an amazing ability to forgive, to heal, and to hope, especially when touched by love.*

CHAPTER ONE

Dust motes floated in the dry, chilly air, winking in the long shafts of winter sunlight that glinted through the attic's dormer window. The soft, yellowy light pooled on the rough plank floor. A lifetime of boxes and bric-a-brac littered every nook along with half a dozen mismatched lamps, a grimy rocking chair, its caning dry-rotted in spots, stacks of leather-bound books, unused furniture pieces, and dozens of other trinkets and gadgets that were once treasured but now looked dated and grubby.

Heather Phillips stood for a moment, listening to the quiet that utterly and completely pervaded the house. She should have become used to it after nearly a month of forced silence, but she had to admit that it was getting to her. Then a faint sound had her tilting her head and she smiled. Even with the house closed up tight against winter's bluster, even all the way up here among the highest bones of The Lonely Loon, Heather could make out the muffled rhythm of the ocean waves.

Two short steps made it possible for her to peer out of the wavy glass of the dormer and see the wide expanse of slate gray water. The boardwalk in front of her B&B and the sandy beach beyond the seawall were both devoid of people at this early hour of the morning. The sea called to her; she suspected it did the same to every single one of the seven thousand or so permanent residents who called Ocean City, Maryland home. During the hot summer months, tourists poured into the town like sweet, luscious lemonade and the population often surpassed a quarter of a million. Jam-packed with vacationers or utterly desolate, the relentless waves took no notice; they kept crashing against the shoreline, day in and day out. A reassuring constancy.

There was something about the Atlantic Ocean that calmed Heather. A deep and abiding *soul serenity* is how she thought of it. True tranquility that couldn't be found any place else on earth. Not for her, at least.

The thoughts made her mouth twist in a wry smirk. This wasn't the time to become bogged down with weighty thoughts. Cathy and Sara, her two best friends in the world, would tease the hell out of her for what they'd deem as silly profundity. The three women were as close as sisters. Closer, really, since Heather knew of quite a few siblings who couldn't stand to be in the same room with each other for more than ten minutes at a time. Friends were your chosen family, of that she was certain.

The mental shake she gave herself was all she needed to get her thoughts back on the right track. Cathy and Sara were stopping by to celebrate tonight. Heather had a thousand things on her to-do list. She'd climbed the narrow attic stairs with a task in mind, and she had better get to it.

Glancing to her right, she spied the boxes of Christmas decorations and made a bee-line for them. Who waits until Christmas Eve to decorate for the holiday?

She shook her head and heaved a sigh. She did. This year, anyway.

Luckily, the outside of the building had been decorated during the first week of December. She'd hired a crew of four men who had painstakingly strung tiny white lights along every straight edge of the building. The electronic icicles that had been installed were a new addition to the decorations this season. Heather had found them in a catalog, and when the long, narrow lights were turned on, they gave the illusion that icicles were actually dripping from the eaves. Thick tubes of red lighting had been coiled around the white columns of the front porch, turning them into fat candy canes, and a huge wreath made of live evergreen branches and sporting a fluffy, red bow greeted visitors at the front door. She breathed in a hefty whiff of pine every time she entered her home. When the house was lit up at night it shouted Christmas spirit, she didn't mind saying.

However, the day the lights had gone up had

also been the day mayhem had broken loose and Heather had discovered just how serious her one and only lodger had been about the peace and quiet he'd felt he had paid for. Heather had been quick to offer reassurances that the job would be completed in one day. And it *had* been, but only because she'd paid the crew overtime *and* a nice bonus so they'd finish up as quickly—and quietly—as possible.

The box at the top of the stack was light but unwieldy. The items inside shifted when she picked it up and she lost her grip. The resulting thud of the box hitting the floor made her eyes grow wide, and she immediately went still, listening for footsteps or shouted complaints from down below.

She realized that her jaw was clenched and her fisted hands were pressed tightly against her solar plexus.

That's when her irritation flared. This tip-toeing around was getting ridiculous. Over the course of the past month she'd learned new habits—turning the knobs when closing doors so the latches wouldn't click, wearing thick socks or slippers so the heels of her shoes didn't tap against the oak floors, listening to her favorite rock and roll station on Pandora with her iPhone and ear buds rather than letting it blare out while she was cooking or cleaning—all for the sake of her guest's expectation of silence.

With a sigh, she quickly let go of her annoyance. As the proprietor of a B&B, she was all too aware that her livelihood depended on her ability and willingness to accommodate the needs of those who came to stay at The Lonely Loon.

"But that doesn't mean I have to like it," she muttered, shoving another box out of her way.

She could groan all she liked, but the truth of the matter was she loved her job. She thoroughly enjoyed meeting and catering to the guests who came to stay at The Loon. Owning and operating her own successful business was a blessing. So many people hated what they did to earn a living. She had the good fortune of enjoying it.

The silver tinsel Christmas tree she'd come for sat behind another large box and Heather wrestled it from its resting place. She owned several fake trees and rotated them each year. The tinsel tree was easy to set up and only required one light bulb.

The small, rotating color panel in the base lit the entire tree. Easy was the way to go this year.

Once she had the tree set up in the great room, she'd come back for the boxes of ornaments and garland. She started down the attic steps, wiggling the six-foot tree this way and that to maneuver it down the narrow stairwell. About halfway down, she stepped on one of the branches. A metal barb poked through her sock and had her yelping. Her other foot slipped on the step, and she landed on her rump with a painful jar that radiated up through the full length of her spine. The tree kept going, thumping down the remaining steps, through the doorway, hitting the hall table like a battering ram, knocking over the brass candlesticks, and sending the angel figurine flying into the air before it hit the floor with a crash, pieces of ceramic skittering across the landing.

A door opened on the floor below, and the sound of heavy footfalls racing up the stairs made Heather groan right out loud. She didn't know what bothered her more, her bruised butt or the trepidation that suddenly swarmed in her chest like a hive of angry wasps. The last thing she needed was a lecture from an irate male.

"What the...?"

As he stood on the third floor landing, he took in the tree, the smashed figurine, the overturned candlesticks. Heather could tell he hadn't seen her sitting on the bottom step of the attic stairs.

She'd never seen eyes like his, color so black it was impossible to tell where the irises ended and the pupils began. And his hair was just as dark, thick, wavy, obsidian locks that hung over his high forehead and the tips of his ears. His features were honed, hawkish even, made sharper by his perpetual frown. He was an unhappy man.

Maybe labeling him like that was unfair. She hardly knew him. Granted, he had been living in the house for nearly a month, but they'd had little contact save for the few moments each morning they'd spent together while she served him breakfast which was almost always done in silence.

Grave? Austere? Focused?

Heather swiped her hair back from her face and the movement drew his attention.

He came closer, skirting the tree that now leaned, cock-eyed, against the hall table. He reached out his hand to her. "You fell down the stairs?"

"Stair," she told him. "Just one. Maybe two. Sorry about the noise."

She took his hand and he helped her to stand. The tiny pinch of pain at the small of her back forced her to wince.

"You're hurt," he said.

"Just my dignity, I'm almost certain," she assured him with a weak smile. It took every ounce of her self-control not to reach around and slide her hand over her bottom to test for tenderness. That would have to wait until later. She tilted her head this way and that, moved her shoulders up and down, shifted her hips. "I think I'm going to live." She attempted to cover her embarrassment with a smile and realized he hadn't released her hand.

His skin was warm and dry, his grip firm, as though he feared she might lose her balance and topple over. His gaze swept over the mess on the hall table, the floor, and the tree.

"What were you thinking?"

Here it comes. She steeled herself for the irate onslaught.

"That thing is huge. Ungainly. I can't believe you tried to move it by yourself."

The kindness in his tone took her off guard.

Completely. And for a second or two, words failed her. He'd been furious the last time a racket had brought him barging out of his room. When he'd come tramping up the stairs, she'd expected him to harangue her again about disturbing his work.

"Are you sure you're all right?" he asked.

Concern softened his eyes, and she could only nod in response.

His gaze swept over the tree again, and he murmured, "I don't think I've ever seen so much tacky tinsel."

"It's pretty when it's lit up," she hurried to assure him. "It turns all sorts of pretty colors. You'll see."

He turned back to her. "It's taller than you are. Heather, really, why didn't you ask me to help you?"

The quiet kindness expressed in his question was her utter undoing. Strangely, tears welled in her eyes, burning like acid, and the knot of emotion that suddenly lodged in her throat made it difficult to speak.

"I'm sorry. I slipped. It's Christmas Eve. I waited as long as I could. I did all the cooking yesterday. That tree isn't tacky. It's vintage. And it takes five minutes to set up. I tried to be quiet. My friends are coming. To celebrate. Tonight. It's *Christmas Eve.* You were so angry about the outside lights. When they went up, I mean." Thinking about it made her spine stiffen. "I wear socks, damn it. I've been tip-toeing around for weeks. I've brought the tree down myself before. But I slipped. I'm sorry."

Was that onslaught coming out of *her* mouth? Was she *babbling*? She wasn't a *babbler.* The whole while all those words were gushing forth, she'd watched his face change. She'd known she needed to shut up, but she couldn't stop her lips from moving or her tongue from flapping.

His lips flattened and he frowned.

In all the weeks he'd been under her roof, she hadn't seen him do anything else.

Heather pulled her hand from his grasp and flicked the tears from her cheeks with her fingers. She blinked. Hard. She took a deep breath and let it out slowly.

"Here, let me get this for you," he said, bending to reach for the tree that leaned against the hall table. "If you're sure you're all right?" He kept his back to her, straightening the tree with one hand, righting the brass candlesticks with the other. Then he stepped over the broken ceramic. "A quick sweep with a broom will have that poor angel cleaned up in no time. I hope it wasn't valuable. I assume you want the tree downstairs? On the main floor? I'll take it wherever you want it. Just say the word."

He moved toward the head of the stairs. Either he was graciously giving her time to regroup, Heather surmised, or her distress made him uncomfortable. Whichever was the case, she was glad to have a chance to pull herself together. She combed her fingers through her hair, took a deep breath, moistened her lips, and moved out onto the hallway landing behind him.

Had she really heard accusation in her tone when she'd gone off on her tangent? Had she really blurted out that she wore socks? As if doing so was some sort of punishment he was causing her? Heather stifled a groan as she reached for the banister.

"Head for the great room, please," she told him. "Thank you, Daniel. I appreciate your help."

Funny how some names just had a too-proper feel to them, and in her opinion, his was one of them. Daniel was formal, a name you might use when someone was, say, winning some sort of important prize, like a Pulitzer or a Nobel. Maybe if he'd asked her to call him Dan or Danny, he would seem less formidable. But he hadn't.

"I'm going to run back to the attic and grab the base of the tree," she told him. "I'll be right behind you."

"Be careful on those stairs," he called over his shoulder.

She held the railing as she hurried up the steps, thinking back to when he'd first arrived, weeks ago on Thanksgiving Day—just as she and her friends were sitting down to dinner, no less. Back then, she'd naturally called him by the name that had been given to her by his agent when the reservation had been made.

D.B. Atwell, famed New York Times bestselling author whose horror books had won a slew of prizes and had been made into more than half a dozen popular films, had rented The Lonely Loon—the *entire* B&B to be precise—for three full months. Seems he was working on a book, and he'd made it clear from that first day that he was looking for peace and quiet in which to write.

Her simple "You'll find plenty of that here,

D.B.," had provoked the first frown of many to pucker his brow.

"Daniel," he'd told her. "Call me Daniel."

So she'd done just as he'd asked; it really didn't matter that his name sounded stiff each time she uttered it. Not that she'd had many chances to use it. Although she saw him each morning when he came down for coffee, the opportunity for conversation was rare due to the manuscript pages, or the yellow legal pad filled with notes, or the map of some foreign country that had held him rapt. The man's intense focus was like that of no one else Heather had ever met. She sometimes wondered, were she to serve him cardboard cutouts rather than scones with his coffee and juice, if he would even notice.

She placed the tree base, the light fixture that would illuminate the tree from underneath, and an extension cord, in a box of other decorations and made her way down the two flights of stairs to the main floor.

"Here we are," Daniel said. He stood in the center of the room. "Can I help you set it up? Where do want it? In the corner?"

"Just lean it against the chair." She set the box on

the floor, and brushed dust from her hands and the front of her dress. "Thank you, but I don't want to bother you any more than I already have. You can go back to work."

He didn't move, not even a smidge. Just stood there looking at her with his arm lost in a sea of silver tinsel. He swung his free hand up to rake at the hair on the back of his head and his expression turned contrite.

"Look, Heather, ah," he began, "it's pretty clear that I've, um..."

He inhaled deeply through his nose, his mouth going rigid.

His wavy hair curled just above the collar of his shirt. His lips were full, his cheekbones high, his jawline sharp. The muscles of his neck stood out in cords when he tipped his head to the side. His eyelids slid shut, hiding his deliciously dark eyes from her, and he swiped his fingers across his mouth.

The man was better than good-looking. He was all dark and mysterious and... *provocative*. That was the word that slipped into her mind. Like Emily Brontë's Heathcliff, or a clean-shaven, Joe Manganiello, only a little swarthier.

The thought made Heather's eyes widen, and she nearly choked on the saliva that had pooled in her mouth while she stood there gawking at him. She immediately averted her gaze. What was the matter with her? She'd been sharing this house with Daniel Atwell for weeks. Why was she just now noticing—

Oh, you didn't just now notice, a little voice in her head intoned. *You've noticed plenty.* She glanced toward the picture window, barely cognizant of the dull gray ocean or the frothy waves churning in the distance.

Ease up. Just because she'd sworn off men and intimate relationships years ago didn't mean she couldn't appreciate a gorgeous guy.

"Listen, Heather," he started again, "I think I need to apologize."

She tipped her chin up a fraction and met his gaze full on. "For what? You've done nothing that warrants an—"

"Wait." He cut her off. "Let me talk a minute. Please."

He shifted his weight and the tinsel quivered.

"Judging from the things you said up there." He lifted both his hand and his gaze toward the ceiling for an instant. "In the hallway, I mean. It seems my need for, um, quiet has caused you... well, for lack of a better word, I guess I'd say I've caused you some frustration. I never imagined that my being here would—"

"Daniel, please." She clasped her hands together and stepped toward him. "I should be the one apologizing. We made a business arrangement, you and I. You needed to get away to finish a book. I'm being paid to provide the quiet place that's necessary for you to do that. I've had to turn away a few regulars, yes, but you've paid me more money than I have ever earned during a winter season."

Heather pressed her lips together, her eyebrows arching. She offered him a quick, lopsided smile. "I probably shouldn't have told you that."

She rubbed her palms together slowly then lowered her hands to her sides before assuring him, "What I'm trying to say is, I knew what I was offering to do. From the start, I knew what you needed. I did. And I had every intention of providing it for you. I still do. Honestly."

His dark gaze took her in.

Before he could speak, she continued, "I'm sorry I ran off at the mouth upstairs. I don't know what's wrong with me." She paused, cocking her head. "Well, that's not quite true. I do know what's wrong. I'm used to socializing, you see. I'm used to having friends around. I'm used to having people in the house. My customers like to chat, to learn about the history of the town, or talk about the best places to eat or shop. All the alone time just started... getting to me." She heaved a sigh. "I guess you used the right word. Clearly, frustration got the better of me. For a moment or two. But I'm okay now. You'll see." She nodded as if to somehow shore up her assurances. "Really."

She finally stopped talking because she couldn't think of another thing to say. The silence that fell between them would have been complete save for the faint, far-off rumbling of the surf.

The tension in his shoulders relaxed and he hooked his thumb into the waistband of his jeans. "I can understand how you're feeling," he said. "A lot of people have trouble with long periods of quiet. I'm actually cognizant of very little of it when I'm working. Quiet, I mean. I have characters talking and moving and interacting in my head. Scenes unfolding. Plots and sub-plots evolving." He shook his head. "Sometimes unraveling. My mind can get so chaotic I'm not even aware of it. Real world silence isn't something I notice. That is, unless it's broken and my work is disturbed."

The idea of conjuring people, situations, whole towns out of nothing but a creative imagination intrigued Heather.

His lips curled into a rare, albeit small, smile as he said, "Most everything you said upstairs made sense. I was able to put the pieces together, I mean. You're planning a little get-together with your friends tonight to celebrate Christmas Eve. You've cooked. You need to decorate."

Then confusion knitted his brow and he drew one cheek muscle back far enough to reveal a dimple she had never seen before.

"But what was that about the socks?" he asked. "You seemed pretty angry about having to wear socks. It's winter. I would think socks would be a good thing. I still can't quite figure out how that fits in with the rest of what you were saying."

Babbling, more like. The thought had her face and neck growing hot.

"Hey," he said softly, "come on now. I didn't mean to embarrass you."

She sighed. "You're not embarrassing me. I've embarrassed myself. Completely and thoroughly."

The deep sound of his chuckle startled Heather and she went still. Then almost immediately she blinked several times and her spine straightened when a warm, pleasant feeling swept though her.

"Okay, okay," he told her. "Let's forget all about the socks. You don't need to explain."

"Oh, yes I do. The complaint was just weird enough that you would never be able to forget, even if you were to try."

Again, he laughed, and that heated sensation thickened and swirled inside her.

Nodding, he murmured, "This is true. So explain quickly. Keep it short and simple. Then we can put it behind us. I promise not to ask any questions."

His teasing only increased the odd feeling that slowly spiraled in her belly.

Heather inhaled deeply. "The heels of my shoes. They click on the oak floors. The stairs. The kitchen tile. I imagined I sounded like an elephant every time I walked across the room."

This time his laughter was hearty enough that dimples appeared in both cheeks now. Heather had already come to the conclusion that he was a handsome man, but now she'd say he was irresistibly appealing—enough to make a girl's toes curl inside her fluffy wool socks.

"You have been going above and beyond, Heather." He shook his head slowly. "And to think I didn't even realize it. I was too busy worrying about—"

He stopped himself suddenly and paused to take a deep breath. Then he softly finished, "I was too busy absorbing all that quiet you were providing." His features went contrite. "I am so sorry. I really am."

In that very instant, she realized that all the frustration and anger and tension that had been building inside her for days and weeks was gone. The air felt relaxed, and she smiled.

"Here," she said, closing the gap between them. "Let me take that tree. It looks like it's about to swallow you whole."

The tinseled branches shuttered when she shifted the tree and leaned it against the high-backed wing chair.

"Thank you for your help, Daniel. I can take it from here. You can get back to your book." She turned toward the box she'd set on the sofa, a wonderful lightheartedness lifting her spirits. "Oh, wait. Before you go. You'll come, won't you? To the party, I mean?"

He stopped in the doorway and faced her. "Thank you, but no. I have work to do. And, besides, I wouldn't want to intrude."

"You're not going to work on Christmas Eve."

He didn't respond, but the mere idea made her sad enough to try again to get him to come.

"You wouldn't be intruding," she insisted. "I'd love for you to meet my friends. And I've cooked a fabulous meal. International dishes from all over the world. It'll be fun."

Although he hesitated, she knew he was about to turn her down again. And if he did, she couldn't really press him further. It wasn't her habit to force her guests to do anything they didn't want to do.

But without thinking, she blurted, "If you agree to come downstairs for the party—" she lifted her hands, palms up "—that means I'll get to wear shoes." She arched her brows. "High heels, even."

Her heart beat once, twice, three times, and she felt breathless as she waited. Then he chuckled. The warm joy that surged in the pit of her gut was more potent than a swallow of brandy on a cold, snowy night.

"When you put it that way," he said, "how can I refuse?"

CHAPTER TWO

This was a mistake. A massive mistake. Probably the worst he'd made since being forced to return to the States six weeks ago.

He had no business celebrating. It didn't matter that millions of people all over the world were gathering together to commemorate one of the holiest and most festive holidays of the year. He was too filled with anxiety and anger and guilt, and every other hellishly dark emotion a human could experience, to put himself in the position of having to appear jovial.

Daniel scanned the room from where he sat at one end of the sofa—the colorful tinsel tree, the crackling fire, the evergreen boughs gracing the mantle with a miniature porcelain family of carolers tucked among the branches whose mouths were frozen mid-song, red felt stockings with silver corded accents hung on hooks, knick-knacky figurines of elves and reindeer and Santa and angels with gossamer wings. Every flat surface was occupied by some sort of holiday decoration. A sprig of mistletoe hung from the top jamb of one of the doorways. Cheery music played in the background. The hearty scents of cinnamon and apple and other delicious, savory smells hung heavy in the air. Clearly, Heather loved to celebrate Christmas.

He was sorry he'd promised her that he'd attend her get-together, but the frustration his need of silence had caused her over the past weeks had him feeling awkwardly ambivalent. He'd stay long enough so as not to be rude, and then he'd make his excuses and return to his room.

"Those meat pies are scrumptious," Heather's

friend Sara said as the two women entered the living room from the dining room.

Heather had said she'd spent yesterday cooking and she hadn't been kidding. The long dining room table was laden with bowls and platters of food.

"Those are beef pasties," Heather told her. "I used an authentic recipe from the UK that I found on-line. I decided on an international menu for tonight. The sweet potato soup is an African recipe. There's tabbouleh salad from Greece, and the hummus and naan are Indian recipes. I have to confess that I bought the naan, but I did bake the maple cookies. That's a Canadian recipe. And, finally, the lemon ricotta pie is from Italy."

Daniel watched her; she was an animated talker. Her blue eyes sparkled and her hands lifted, turned, and fanned out, expressing a warmth and eagerness to engage.

Then unwittingly his gaze traveled down the length of her. She wore a deep red, high-necked dress made of some thin fabric, silk maybe. The waist was cinched by a wide black leather belt, and the full skirt flowed over her lush, curvy hips and fell to mid-calf. The outfit had a unique look, a style he should recognize but couldn't put a name to. He noticed that the wide sleeves ended in a distinctive point at the backs of her hands, and then it came to him. The dress looked like a garment from the Renaissance Period.

And she looked stunning in it.

The silent observation rushed him, left him astonished. Confounded. He sat there, frowning, as a distinctly rare but familiar feeling of desire sparked to life in him, warming the ice water that had been flowing through his veins and chilling his body for longer than he could remember.

"Well, look at you! An international meal. It's perfect." Sara offered Heather a wide smile. Then Sara turned her attention to Daniel. "Have you eaten? Everything I've tried is delicious."

He nodded and smiled, giving himself time to find his tongue.

"I had some soup before you arrived," he said. "And more than my share of those maple cookies, I'm sure." He lifted his mug. His arms felt lanky, disjointed, as if they didn't belong to him. "The apple cider is really good. Have you tried it?"

He pressed his lips together, grinding his jaw. Every sip he enjoyed was like a guitar pick, twanging the taut strings of guilt inside him. He shouldn't be having a good time. He shouldn't be noticing how the fabric of Heather's dress hugged her curves. He shouldn't be participating in pleasantries. It wasn't fair to Mia.

He wanted to bolt, but he forced himself to remain in his seat. This was important to Heather, he reminded himself. Just a little longer and he could retreat upstairs.

"I forgot about the cider, Sara." Heather pointed to the table set up near the bay window. "That's a good, old Colonial American recipe. I've put it in a crock pot to keep it warm."

Sara was one of Heather's best friends. She ran the bakery downstairs that was aptly named Sara's Sweet Shop, and Daniel had gone down a time or two. The molasses cookies she offered for sale were especially good with a cup of hot tea on cold winter afternoons.

"I think I'll have some cider." Sara skirted the wing chair as she crossed the room.

"Help yourself," Heather told her. "There's wine there, if you'd rather have something stronger."

"Cider sounds good, thanks." Then she called out, "Landon, come have some cider."

Landon Richards was Sara's significant other. He did odd jobs at the B&B. Nearly every time Daniel had seen the man around the house, Landon was usually carrying a toolbox or plumber's tape or paint brushes.

"Be there in a sec," Landon answered from the dining room. "Having a second helping of this salad."

"Poor man," Sara told them, ladling fragrant cider into a cup. "He's been delivering meals to the elderly all day. He's volunteering for Meals On Wheels. He had so many people to see, he didn't get a chance to stop for lunch." She inhaled the steam rising from her cup and then took a sip. "Mmmm. So good." Sara cradled the cup between her palms. "I hope Cathy's okay. She should have been here by now."

"I haven't heard from her all day," Heather said. "But then I've been busy."

The front door opened out in the foyer and Heather and Sara grinned at each other.

"Speak of the devil," Heather said.

"Yoo-hoo!" A huge puff of chilled air rolled into the room along with Cathy's greeting. She appeared in the doorway of the living room, her arms laden with brightly wrapped packages. "Can someone help me, please?"

Heather rushed forward.

"I met a family out on the boardwalk, Heather," Cathy said, her tone hushed, her words swift. "The little girl loves The Loon. I invited them to come inside and warm up. I knew you'd have a fire going. I hope it's not a prob—"

"Are you kidding me?" Heather brushed aside Cathy's concern with a wide, warm smile. "More people means more fun."

In an instant, Daniel's ambivalence grew to monster proportions. Heather was certainly enjoying this unexpected surprise; he just hoped he could find the right moment to make good his escape.

A little girl of about nine or ten came into the room. Pale and delicate looking, her dark eyes seemed abnormally large. It took a second or two for Daniel to figure out why...

Her head was bald and as glossy as a polished pearl. Obvious signs of harsh medical treatment. For cancer. Her parents followed her from the foyer, but Daniel's attention remained riveted to the child. Her gaze latched onto the tinseled tree and she gasped softly in wonder.

"It's beautiful." As if in a sleep-walker trance, she ambled over to the tree, coming to a halt mere inches from the glowing silver.

Daniel took a moment to look toward Heather. Her blue eyes glistened with moisture and her smile had faded. Then he glanced at Cathy and Sara, and saw that both women tried valiantly to mask the tender sympathy that nearly overwhelmed them.

The girl was sick, that much was evident. Her veins showed blue beneath her milky skin where it was thinnest, her neck, her temples, her scalp, and crescent-moon-shaped shadows stained the area beneath her huge eyes. Even her supraorbital arch looked oddly accentuated as whatever medical treatment she was enduring had robbed her of her eyebrows.

Cancer could wreak havoc on the human body, and to see someone so young having to deal with such a serious illness... Daniel felt a knot rise in his throat. It was woefully tragic.

Her mother followed close on her heels and

squatted down next to her. "I've never seen anything quite as pretty."

"Everyone," Cathy said after clearing her throat, "this is my new friend, Izzie. This is her mom and dad, and I invited them in for some apple cider by the fire so they can warm up a bit. It is cold out there tonight."

Introductions were made, and Daniel watched Heather's face light up when she learned just how much Izzie loved The Lonely Loon.

"It's my very favorite place on the boardwalk." She darted a quick smile at her dad, and together they said, "During winter."

The two of them laughed.

Aaron, Izzie's father, explained, "Her summer favorite is the arcade."

Her mom, Christy, just stood there, beaming.

"Mine too!" Heather reached out and touched Izzie's shoulder affectionately. "I like skee-ball. How about you?"

"Air hockey."

"Now you're talking," Sara chimed in. "I am an air hockey champion."

Cathy handed Izzie a cup of cider. "I like the shooting gallery, myself."

"Oh, that's fun, too," Izzie said.

"There's food in the dining room," Heather said. "Are you hungry?"

Watching the women fawn over the child caused a walnut-sized lump to form in Daniel's throat. At the same time, Izzie's dark, haunting eyes reminded him so keenly of Mia that he felt as if an army of termites had taken up residence under his skin. The need to squirm made it nearly impossible for him to sit still.

Sara passed around a plate of cookies she'd brought in from the dining room. Landon joined the group and another round of introductions ensued. Silent Night played from the speakers, and Izzie began to softly sing. One by one, the adults joined her... all of them except Daniel. He didn't trust his voice not to crack like cheap glass.

What are you doing tonight, Mia? Are you laughing? Eating cookies? Opening gifts? Singing carols?

The questions whispered through his mind like a sharp, salty breeze rolling through dune grass.

Who are you with? Where are you, sweetheart?

The song ended, and he felt the sheen of sweat that had broken out across his forehead and upper lip. The party guests mingled and laughed as yet

35

another jazzy Christmas tune began to play in the background. Surely, he'd made a polite showing. Heather was busy enough with her other guests that she wouldn't be offended if he were to slip away.

He placed his hands firmly on his knees and had every intention of rising, but then Izzie was suddenly standing in front of him.

"Is it okay if I sit down for a while?"

"Of course it's okay." Even though there was plenty of room, he slid over an inch or two to make her feel welcome.

She settled on the sofa, not on the other end but in the center, right next to him. She smiled up at him.

"You look sad."

Her innocent honesty stunned him.

"I am a little," he confessed. "You see, I'm missing someone. Someone special."

She nodded her bald head. "Yeah, me too. I miss my mom really bad."

Daniel couldn't keep the frown from planting itself on his forehead. He glanced over at the adults he'd assumed were Izzie's parents.

"Oh, she's not my mom," Izzie said quietly.

"She's a stand in. She's a nurse at the hospital where I get my treatments."

His frown deepened, and although his curiosity urged him to ask Izzie what she'd meant about the woman being a "stand in," he remained silent. As a writer, he talked to people in order to learn about their jobs, their personal expertise, their life adventures, and more often than not, he ended up incorporating the knowledge and experiences into his works of fiction. He'd learned over the years to keep his mouth shut as much as possible. It was a rule that, when followed, warranted the greatest amount of information.

He hoped his nod would encourage her to continue to elaborate.

"Hey," Izzie said softly, "do you think it's wrong for me to wish for Santa to make my daddy and Christy get married?"

Daniel's frown disappeared as his eyebrows arched high. This kid offered one surprise after another. He licked his lips and cleared his throat to give himself a few seconds to think about how he should respond.

"Well..." he began. He looked at Izzie's father

then back at Izzie. Rather than answer her question, Daniel asked one of his own.

"That's on your wish list for Santa?"

"It's not actually written down," she admitted. "Yet." She grinned. "I didn't know if Daddy could find anyone to come with us to Ocean City."

"I see." But he really didn't.

"I do have a list in my journal. I have it memorized. Wanna hear?"

The excitement sparkling in her brown eyes was contagious.

"Absolutely. I'd love to hear."

"I'm asking Santa for all the things that make a perfect Christmas," she said. "And I think I just might get them. I want a tree with pretty lights. We already got one of those. And Christmas carols. We just sung one." She ticked the items off on her fingers. "I want to have my picture taken with Santa. I want lots of cookies. And presents. And snow." She took a moment to look up at him. "I *really* want snow. And a make-believe mommy. That's what Christy is doing. Standing in for my mommy 'cause my mommy died a long time ago."

Izzie studied his face for a moment. "A family is

just better with a mommy *and* a daddy, don't you think?"

Her query was both pointed and poignant, and he knew exactly what she meant.

The more the child revealed, the more questions formed in Daniel's head. And the more his heart felt like it was being squeezed by a huge fist. Life had dealt this poor little girl more than her share of tragedy.

Just like his Mia.

Hot tears burned his eyes. He swallowed around the lump that had now taken up residence in his throat and forcibly blinked away his tears. He refused to surrender to despair. Mia would be found. She would be brought home to him. He had to hold onto those thoughts or he risked losing his sanity completely.

His voice was raspy when he told Izzie, "I hope Santa brings you the perfect Christmas you're looking for."

The little girl smiled, suddenly looking as weary as he felt.

"Thanks, mister."

CHAPTER THREE

"Happy New Year!" Heather, Sara, and Cathy shouted the three words boisterously along with hoots and hollers and laughter. It didn't matter that they were standing in the narrow alley behind The Lonely Loon. Nor did it matter that midnight had come and gone, and that they were old enough to know better than to act like half raised heathens. But the rum runners they'd enjoyed at Seacrets had removed every ounce of their caring.

The nightclub had been loud and crowded and full of energy that could only be described as happy, vivacious, and totally infectious.

"Wow, I needed this!" Heather pulled Sara and Cathy to her and wrapped her arms around them for a group hug. "You have *no idea*."

"Oh, I think we do," Sara said, laughing.

Heather hugged them tight. "Thanks for dropping me off."

Cathy cupped her hands around her mouth and yelled, "Thanks, Landon."

Heather leaned away from Cathy. "Hey, that's my hearing you're ruining there."

Sara's Landon had acted as their designated driver for the evening. He waited in the car out on the street for Sara and Cathy, keeping the engine humming and the heater running.

"He's been such a good sport tonight," Sara murmured. "He needs a special wish."

Without hesitation, all three of them turned toward the street and shouted, "Happy New Year, Landon!"

Then Cathy murmured, "Sara, you'll give him something special when you get home, right? We want him to know how much we appreciate his services."

"You can bet your sweet bippy, I will," Sara promised.

"Bippy?" Heather asked, her head a little dizzy, her heart very happy. "I haven't heard that word in decades. What the hell *is* a bippy, anyway?"

"It's an unspecified part of the anatomy," Cathy said.

Heather and Sara both turned their heads slowly and looked at Cathy as if she'd grown a third eye in the center of her forehead.

"What?" Cathy threw her shoulders back. "Hey, I watch Jeopardy, you know!"

Sara snickered, and then all three of them laughed so hard Cathy snorted, and that made them laugh all over again.

A dog barked, and a light flickered on in a window of one of the neighboring buildings.

"Shhh. Quiet." Even though she continued to chuckle, Heather lifted her hands, trying to quell the humor that glittered and flared between them like sparklers.

"Yes, we should tone it down." Sara shifted her pretty silver clutch to her other hand.

Cathy nodded. "The last thing we need is to get arrested for disturbing the peace."

But then their mischievous gazes met, and danced.

"That might be the perfect way to ring in the New Year."

"Cathy, as fun as that sounds, we can't ask Landon to bail us out of jail." Sara shook her head. "He would not be amused."

Movement at the corner of the house made them all go quiet. When the man stepped into the moonlight, Heather could see it was Daniel. He walked toward the back door of the B&B, his head bent, his shoulders hunched against the night chill, his hands stuffed into the pockets of his jacket.

"Speaking of not being amused..." Heather let the rest of the thought trail as she stared toward the shadows that obscured the back door from her view.

"Oh, nothing could amuse that man," Cathy chimed in. "He's a real grump that Daniel Atwell is."

"Maybe he went out, after all," Sara offered brightly. Sara's glass was almost always half-full. "To a pub or something."

"No way." Cathy swiped her hand through the air for emphasis. "That one is allergic to people. And celebrations. And fun of any kind."

"Come on now," Heather chided. "He's not that bad."

Cathy crossed her arms, her mouth twisting into a stubborn purse.

"As much as I hate to do it, I think I have to agree with Cath on this one," Sara said. "What kind of man doesn't celebrate the holidays? I mean, he sat in the corner at the Christmas Eve party, barely speaking to anyone. Then he disappeared without a word. And you said he turned down your invitation to go out tonight."

"He did, yes." Heather's chin dipped when she nodded slowly. "But you know how that goes." She lifted her shoulders in a shrug. "Some people just aren't... sociable. That doesn't mean there's anything wrong with him. He's a perfectly nice man."

"Once again," Cathy said, "you're being too kind, Heather. 'Not sociable' doesn't even touch the surface with him. You've said so yourself. He barely comes out of his room. He lives like a hermit."

The magnitude of sympathy that welled up inside Heather surprised her. She loved her friends dearly, but she couldn't help feeling they were being just a little unfair.

"I did not use the word hermit. He does come down for breakfast," she told them. "He's been to the café once or twice, Cathy. And the sweet shop, too. I know he has because he always leaves me a few cookies on the kitchen table." As an afterthought, she added, "And he takes walks." Then she murmured, "Lots of walks."

"Alone," Sara pointed out. "He's always so alone. And miserable. At least, that's what it looks like. It's just not normal."

"He does have a job to do." Heather could hear the defensiveness in her voice and it made her uncomfortable. "He's focused on his work."

"Oh, just stop it already," Cathy said. "He's writing a book. How hard can *that* be?"

"You, my dear..." Heather arched a brow at Cathy "...are drunk."

"Speaking of writing a book..." Sara grinned unabashedly. "I'm thinking of putting together a cookbook."

Heather was relieved to have a change of subject,

and she and Cathy both happily encouraged Sara to tell them more.

"I'm thinking of calling it Patty Cake and Cupcakes. It'll focus on desserts, of course."

Looking at Sara's wide-eyed, smiling face, Heather loved seeing her friend radiating with so much joy. Landon had made an amazing change in her life.

"I think it's a wonderful idea," Cathy said. "Why haven't you said something? We could have batted around ideas."

Sara averted her gaze, but only for a split second. She reached to tuck a strand of hair behind her ear, lifting her eyes first to Cathy, and then to Heather.

That one, quick moment of hesitation was all it took to start Heather's mind spinning. "Wait a minute," she murmured. "Sara...? Patty Cake?"

Cathy gasped. "Are you pregnant?"

Clearly panicked, Sara shook her head. "No. No. I didn't say that. Did I say that?"

Heather squinted and her tone was tinged with slight accusation as she said, "You know, now that I think about it, you didn't have a single rum runner tonight. I bought the first round and Cathy ended up drinking yours."

"That's right," Cathy said. "You carried around a glass of white wine all evening long. And I never saw you ask for a refill."

"And here I was," Heather harrumphed, "thinking we were all getting tipsy together."

Judging from her expression, Sara knew she'd been snared. Where just seconds before she had been beaming with happiness, now her forehead was marred with worry; the anxiety had even etched itself around her mouth.

She pressed her lips together for the span of two heartbeats, clearly trying to decide how much to reveal, and then she whispered. "You can't say anything about this. I mean it. I don't know for sure." Then she admitted, "But I *am* late."

Heather and Cathy hooted and grabbed at her, hopping up and down in their excitement.

"But you can't say anything," Sara stressed again. "I didn't mean to open my big mouth. I need to make sure first. I can't say anything until I'm certain. It's only fair that I tell Landon first."

"Our lips are sealed," Heather promised.

"What do you think he's going to say?" Cathy asked.

"I don't know." Sara's frowned deepened.

"Aw, don't worry," Heather reassured her. "Things are good between you. He loves you, Sara."

"Do you think he'll want to get married?" Cathy asked.

"I honestly don't know." Sara's panic quickly escalated.

"Okay, okay." Cathy placed her hand on Sara's shoulder to calm her. "I'll stop with the questions. It'll all be fine."

"I might not say this often, but she's right," Heather said, touching Sara's forearm. "Everything is going to be just fine."

Cathy clenched her fists and shimmied her shoulders. Excitement shook her words as she whispered, "We're going to have a baby!"

Arching her brows at Sara, Heather warned, "She might have a bit of a problem containing herself."

"Not a word to Landon, Cathy." Sara pointed a stern finger at her friend. "Not unless you want a bippy beating."

~*~

Heather slipped through the back door of the house, not totally surprised to see Daniel sitting at the kitchen table. The scent of vanilla chamomile tea wafted in the air.

"Hi," she greeted. "You okay?"

He nodded. "Just couldn't sleep."

She knew she should excuse herself, tell him goodnight, and slip off to bed. He liked his solitude. But the excitement of the New Year celebration still pulsed through her. She'd never be able to fall asleep yet no matter how hard she tried. "Is the water still hot? Do you mind if I have a cup of tea with you?"

Even worse than not going to bed when she highly suspected he'd rather be alone, she didn't wait for him to answer either question before turning on her heel and going to the cabinet for a mug. While she busied herself getting a teabag and pouring still-steaming water from the pot, she was overly aware of his silence.

She didn't agree with Cathy that Daniel was a grump. He could be perfectly gracious, even pleasant, when he wanted to be. However, she did believe Sara was right in her assessment that the poor man seemed very much alone and miserable.

Unhappiness radiated off him like heat from a bonfire, and she wished she could do something about it. Help him in some way. Maybe offer him a sympathetic ear, or a shoulder to lean on.

But how could she make such an offer when she knew down to the bone that he wasn't the type of man who would want such an overture? The quandary had her brows knitting together.

"I want to assure you..."

His voice jarred the quiet like the clash of cymbals and she started.

"...that I'm not allergic to people."

Horrified, she turned around to face him. "Oh, Daniel. You heard us."

He stared down into the ceramic mug, his thumb lightly tapping the handle. "I didn't eavesdrop on purpose." He lifted his gaze to hers. "I had trouble with the key. I've been meaning to tell you that my back door key sticks."

"I'm sorry." She moistened her lips. "We shouldn't have been talking about you like that."

One corner of his mouth quirked upward. "The acoustics in that alley are amazing. I tried to get inside as quickly as I could. But I wasn't fast enough to keep from hearing the word miserable applied to me."

Heather's shoulders rounded. "Oh, Daniel," she repeated, shaking her head. She'd already apologized; she didn't know what else to say.

"I *am* miserable," he said softly. "Sick with misery, actually. You see, I didn't want to write this damned book. I didn't want to be cloistered away. Not right now when... well, not right now."

Her tea forgotten, she crossed the room, slid out a chair, and sat down next to him at the table. She was amazed by his admission, astonished that he was actually confiding in her.

She reached out and slipped her fingers over his taut forearm, and she was immediately aware of the heat emanating from him through the soft cotton of his shirtsleeve.

"Not this time of year. But I didn't have a choice, Heather."

Her eyes were drawn to his clenched jaw muscle.

"And contrary to what was said out there in the alley, I'm just as much a social creature as the next guy."

"I am so sorry your feelings were hurt. We'd been drinking, you see. That tends to loosen our tongues. We say things we shouldn't." It was a feeble explanation at best.

"It's okay. I'm not the thinned-skinned type." He patted the back of her hand. "You can't be a writer and allow yourself to be easily offended. There are literary critics who would love to flay me alive if they could." He looked toward the ceiling and wearily whispered, "Everyone has a right to an opinion."

She realized that his palm still rested on her hand, his fingertips slipping beneath the cuff of her blouse. The pads of his index and middle fingers lightly rubbed back and forth across her wrist. Of course, he was lost in what he was saying, preoccupied with his thoughts, and completely unaware that he was touching her so intimately.

But every nuance of her attention became focused on the slight friction of his skin against hers, her heart skittering in her chest, her rising temperature making her feel the need to draw air into her lungs a little faster, a little deeper.

"Anyway..."

When he spoke, she looked him in the eyes and saw humor dancing there.

"...you have no reason to apologize," he said,

firmly. "You took up for me out there, and I thank you for that. I just needed you to know that I'm not the kind of man your friends think I am. And I wouldn't be here over the holidays if I had any other choice. I'd much rather be celebrating the holidays with my little girl."

He has a daughter. Heather suddenly felt weak.

"If I could be with her," he continued, "I would be. But that's impossible right now."

She *knew* he was unhappy, knew he had been struggling with something heavy, something extremely stressful, and now the reason had been revealed; he was spending the holidays away from his child. That would be enough to make anyone gloomy and sad.

"So now that I've confessed and it's out in the open," he said, "tell me about your evening."

"But... don't you want to talk a little more about what's going on with you? It must be very upsetting for you. Being away from your daughter."

He shook his head. "To tell you the honest truth, Heather, I took a walk tonight to clear the bad thoughts from my head. If I start talking about it, I won't rest at all. I'd rather let you talk. Tell me, did you have a good time with your friends?"

The sharp turn in the conversation blindsided her. If she could help him quiet his mind by telling him about her evening out, she would do it. Before she had time to think, she was murmuring, "Well, I had as good a time as I could. Being a fifth wheel, and all."

"A fifth wheel? I was under the impression that it was going to be a girls' night."

She regretted the statement as soon as it passed her lips. His eyes, the color of onyx, were pensive, intensely curious.

"Well," she began slowly, "Sara's Landon was our designated driver, so he was with us. And Bradley showed up unexpectedly. He's, well," she drew out the word, "a friend of Cathy's. Not a friend, exactly, but more like..."

Cathy's relationship with Brad was peculiar to say the least. Too close to be mere friends, yet not close enough to have earned a more intimate label. Cathy, Sara, and Heather were always at odds over how to describe it. Best buddies with benefits? The "with benefits" fit just fine, but the "best buddies" did not. The two of them were so on again, off again. Heather decided it would be best to put an end to the commentary right then and there.

Daniel didn't need to know all the sordid details of Cathy's love life.

Lust life, more like. Heather bit her lip to keep from grinning.

"*Anyway*," Heather stressed, "the point I was trying to make is that Sara was with someone, and so was Cathy. And I was—"

"The fifth wheel," he finished for her. "Got it. I can see how that wouldn't be much fun."

"The worst of it was the stroke of midnight." She sighed. "Everyone got a New Year's kiss but me."

"Well, that's not quite fair, now is it?"

The tone of his voice had her gaze lifting to connect with his. Merriment sparkled in his eyes. Was he laughing at her? Poking fun?

She slid her fingers from between his forearm and hand, meaning to pull away from him, from the situation that could very quickly turn both awkward and embarrassing for her. Feeling vulnerable was not something she enjoyed. She mentally kicked herself for not keeping the conversation light and fluffy. That's what he'd expected, wasn't it? It's the only kind of conversation that most guys liked. Nothing too intense. Nothing too sensitive. Frivolous. Insignificant. Superficial. That's what—

He reached out and captured her jaw between his gentle fingers, and she went stock still. With light, steady pressure, he guided her toward him. With excruciating slowness, he leaned forward.

He was close, so close she could feel his warm, vanilla scented breath against her cheek.

What the hell was he doing? She should stop this. She should place her hand on his shoulder and give a good, hard push. But her muscles had gone all spongy and useless. She had no idea what he planned to do, but every cell in her body wanted him to do it.

Daniel tipped up her chin and closed the small gap between them.

His lips were soft and hot against hers. The kiss was—

...over before she had a chance to really enjoy it.

"Everyone deserves a New Year's kiss."

His silky soft voice sent shivers spiraling down the full length of her body. She felt giddy, and drunker than any rum runner could ever account for.

"Ha...Happy New Year," she stammered.

Before she could finish, his mouth was on hers again. This kiss was longer, more lingering, and teetered on the edge of hungry.

When he broke away, Heather heard a strange whooshing, and she realized it was the sound of her blood throbbing at a wild rate through her veins. She swallowed, exhaled slowly, and blinked.

He smiled broadly. "*That*," he told her, "was for telling your friends that I'm perfectly nice."

CHAPTER FOUR

Several days into the New Year, Daniel paced the confines of the bedroom. He would pause every so often and stare out the window at the wide expanse of platinum gray ocean. A thick blanket of clouds hovered in an ashen sky. Heavy. Bleak. Gloomy. Dispiriting. Just like his mood. He'd never felt so damned helpless in his life.

Each day seemed to stretch into an eternity. The book was a useful distraction. Usually, he could become lost in the writing of the story, at least for a good, solid chunk of time. The hours he spent creating characters and plotting out scenes offered his mind a respite from worry. But no matter how hard he tried to work, no matter how many times he sat down in front of his laptop, today the words simply refused to come. He'd even slipped on his lucky orange socks, the ones that always demolished the wall of writer's block. But this time... nothing. He felt that, if he didn't get out of this room and breathe some fresh air, he would lose his mind.

He picked up his wallet from the bedside table and shoved it into his back pocket. The antsy feeling plaguing him made his skin itch. Snatching up his keys, he headed for the door.

The usual solitary walk on the beach or the length of the boardwalk was not going to help. He couldn't abide the thought of being alone. His thoughts of Mia were a jumble of anxious chaos, and his imagination conjured up all manner of bad happenings across the ocean. The turmoil would soon send him into a tailspin. The day—and his mood—were too utterly dismal. He needed some company.

The soles of his shoes tapped against the oak

steps as he made his way downstairs and he found himself shaking his head, remembering Heather's claim of wearing socks so as not to disturb him. She was such a sweet soul. He circled through the house, living room, foyer, dining room, library. He'd gotten to know The Lonely Loon well during his five week stay.

Five weeks. How the hell could this nightmare have gone on for five long weeks?

He found Heather in the kitchen, sitting at the table, her head bobbing slightly in time with whatever music was filtering through the ear buds she was wearing. He paused in the doorway to watch her work. She gave the silver plate she was polishing her undivided attention. Who polished silver these days? People who took pride in their possessions, he guessed.

Heather was such a beautiful woman. Light from the fixture on the ceiling glinted off her shiny brown hair. A sturdy, plastic clip secured about half of it at the back of her head, but the rest curled softly around her shoulders and spilled down her back. The urge to remove the clip, to comb his fingers through her hair, welled up in him, clear and sharp. He loved seeing her in the morning as she served breakfast, her thick mane flowing around her like a winter cape.

Her vivid blue eyes twinkled with—

His spine straightened and he was taken aback when he realized she was looking at him. Without disconnecting her gaze from his, she set the plate on the towel-draped table, dropped her polishing cloth, and tugged the buds from her ears.

"I'm sorry," she said. "Were you trying to get my attention? I guess I have this music turned up too loud."

"No, no," he assured her. "No need to apologize. I, ah, just got here."

Her mouth formed a silent 'oh' and she nodded slowly. He got the distinct idea that she didn't quite believe him. And why should she? He'd been standing here for at least a couple of minutes watching her.

"So, what can I do for you?"

Her lips curled into a broad smile that further disarmed him.

"I, um, I, uh," he stammered. "Well, I guess you could say that, uh, I'm not having the best of days."

"I'm sorry to hear that."

"I know this is going to seem like an out-the-ordinary request. I've been avoiding the company of others since I arrived." He licked his lips. "But I was hoping you could provide me with a... hmmm, let's call it a diversion." He offered her a lopsided grin and added, "You know, some female companionship."

Time seemed to crawl forward as her expression slowly metamorphosed—her smile slipped, then disappeared altogether, her brows drew together, then a full-fledged frown bit deeply between her eyes. Her gaze went shadowy and he could tell she was doing some fast and furious thinking.

"Well, I guess I could try," she finally murmured.

It was almost as if she were speaking to herself.

"But I have to admit," she said, her tone stronger, "in all the years I've run this place, I've been asked to provide some odd things, but no one has ever asked for a lady of the evening."

The phrase she used made Daniel's head jerk a fraction and he blinked. In an instant, it was as though his brain short-circuited. Words wouldn't come. Oh, plenty of them bounced around in his mind like a dozen ping pong balls, but he couldn't quite get his tongue or lips to move so he could actually utter them.

"To tell you the truth," she continued, "I wouldn't even know where to find one. You only want one, right? I mean, is there some sort of service I call, or a certain part of town I should visit?"

"No." The tiny word came out sounding as if he'd just finished running a marathon. He feared she might be thinking he was actually answering her questions and his anxiety shot through the roof. He shook his head from side to side. "No, no, no."

His overly-animated reaction clearly confused her and she went still.

"No lady of the evening." He shook his head again, knowing his voice was way too loud, but there was nothing to be done about that. Then he took a deep breath. The quicker he got this rush of panic under control, the quicker he could make her understand. "That's not what I meant."

Relief softened her entire demeanor. Her shoulders lowered a full inch, and her facial muscles relaxed. She repositioned the cloth that sat on the silver plate, and when she next looked at him, she pressed her lips together, her cheeks flushing pink.

"Clearly I misunderstood," she whispered. "I apologize."

She looked away, and he thought she was embarrassed. But then her eyes went all shiny and she flattened her mouth again in an attempt to hold back her humor.

Laughter rolled out of him like a mighty explosion. It came from deep in his chest, way down in his belly, the sound big and round, and he lifted his face to the ceiling and let it out. He laughed for a good, long time, until his eyes watered and his cheeks ached, and Heather joined him.

"Oh, wow," he said when he was finally able to catch his breath, "that felt so good."

"I really am sorry, Daniel."

He waved off her words. "No apologies necessary. I needed that. Badly." He inhaled and exhaled deeply, feeling better with the release of tension. He couldn't remember when he'd last been overwhelmed with genuine laughter.

Daniel crossed his arms over his chest and leaned against the door jam. "I would like some female companionship, but only for dinner. I promise you." He offered her a wry grin.

She nodded and then reached up to tap her chin. "Cathy and Brad are still on the outs. I could call her to see if she's free for—"

"*You*, Heather." He balanced his weight squarely on both his feet and leaned toward her. "I'm asking you to have dinner with me."

"Oh."

For half a second, he could see that the notion hadn't entered her head.

Then she smiled. "Well, why didn't you just say that from the beginning? You'll start thinking I'm an idiot, and I'm not. I swear to you."

"I take full responsibility for your confusion." He shrugged. "What can I say? I'm a writer. I use twenty-five words when five will suffice. So what do you say? Will you be my diversion for the evening?"

She beamed like a ray of warm, summer sunlight. "I'd love to."

~*~

They enjoyed dinner at Fager's Island. Heather ordered the pan seared Atlantic salmon, and the succulent fish arrived with fluffy mashed potatoes and steamed broccoli. Daniel devoured his Maryland style crab cake, served with rice pilaf and seasoned, roasted root veggies. They both enjoyed a local craft beer.

Heather had suggested Fager's because she loved the jazz band that often entertained there. The sax player could tease out notes that made you break out in goose flesh. She knew the music, the delicious food, and the moonlight shining on the bay water that was black as squid ink would surely help Daniel forget whatever was troubling him, at least for a while. And that's just what had happened.

Their dinner conversation remained casual, light. Inconsequential banter, really. She told him how, over the years, she'd seen businesses come and go along the boardwalk, that she felt grateful that people continued to return to her B&B, and how many of her visitors recommended her to their friends who were looking for a relaxing, laid-back vacation experience. He'd likened his own career to hers, at least in the repeat-customer area; he had people who bought and read each new publication, and many of them recommended his stories to other avid readers.

"Sometimes," he'd said, "people don't realize the power of word-of-mouth recommendations. You know... you tell two friends and they tell two friends..." He'd swiped his crisp, white napkin across his dusky lips. "It keeps people like you and me working and earning a living."

Heather had nodded, holding his gaze intently. "That's so true. It's good when people talk. If they're saying good things, that is."

She'd felt a warm tendril of connection curl in her belly, but then he'd glanced over at the band, enjoying the music for several moments, and Heather concluded that the warmth she'd felt must be the result of the alcohol in the glass of wine she'd consumed.

They'd left the restaurant in mid-town and had driven home, but rather than calling it a night, Daniel had asked her to walk with him.

Although the temperature was edged with the chill of January, the air was utterly still. Heather had turned up the collar of her coat, and the soft scarf tucked securely around her neck kept her plenty warm. Sparse grains of sand grated between the soles of their shoes and the wood planks as they strolled south on the boardwalk.

"So," he said, "there's something I've been dying to ask you."

He spoke softly, and Heather tilted her head toward him.

"What kind of crazy requests have you gotten from your guests," he asked, "that would have you concluding that I was looking for a prostitute?"

A humorous lilt lightened his tone, and Heather hoped her chuckle covered the flush of embarrassment that rushed to her face.

"Oh, you'd be surprised. I once arranged for a male stripper to come for a bachelorette party. That was a wild evening, I don't mind saying." She stuffed her fists deeper into the pockets of her coat. "I had a guest who wanted a milk bath once."

He stopped walking and turned to face her. "You mean, like Cleopatra?"

"Exactly."

"Did you do it?"

"I did. And she paid a hefty price for the luxury, too. I bought the fifty-two gallons of milk, but I hired someone to heat it and carry it upstairs. That was the most expensive and luxurious soak she ever took, I'm sure."

He thought for a moment and then murmured, "Wow."

She laughed. "That's what I said... all day long."

They continued their walk toward the inlet.

"I've chartered a boat for a couple who wanted to scatter their dog's ashes at sea. I went out and bought seventeen feather pillows for a guest who had a bad back." She pursed her lips a moment while she thought. "One man pulled a prank on his wife that included filling their room with two hundred and seven plastic flamingos. Thank goodness, he bought the birds weeks ahead of time and had them shipped to The Loon. I stored them until the couple arrived, and I decorated their room while they were out to lunch one day. I had to ask Sara and Cathy to help me in order to finish up in the hour and a half he gave me."

Again, Daniel stopped and looked at her. This time, his head tilted and his gaze narrowed.

"Don't ask me what was so special about the number two hundred and seven. Or what the flamingos were all about, either." She lifted her hands and offered a grin. "I never did find out, so I have no idea. All I do know is that the woman was absolutely delighted. After she found the flamingos, they acted like a couple of lovesick teenagers."

He chuckled.

"Then there was the Mariachi band," she told him. "A guest wanted to propose to his girlfriend accompanied by authentic Mexican music." One corner of her mouth curled upward. "Not knowing any Mariachi musicians, I called the Chamber of Commerce for some ideas. They put me in touch with a local Mexican restaurant that featured a weekly Mariachi night."

Her smile widened as she remembered the band members' colorful costumes, wide-brimmed sombreros, and lively music.

"That girl squealed like a kid, and then she cried." Heather shook her head slowly, her voice going soft, as she continued, "Just imagine, you're lying out on the beach in your bikini, and suddenly you're surrounded by a loud, flamboyant, singing trio. It's enough to bring anyone to tears."

The thought had her chuckling, but her humor waned when she watched Daniel's mouth go flat.

"Not something I can imagine," he said, his tone deadpan. "Me... in a bikini."

They both laughed then.

She gave his shoulder a nudge with hers. "You know what I meant."

He nodded. "I did. But I couldn't resist teasing you. I love how your cheeks turn rosy."

They came to the end of the boardwalk and Daniel reached out to rest his palms on the white picket fencing. Heather took in the scene before her and felt her shoulder muscles relax. Thin wispy clouds partially covered the half moon that hung over the water like a thirsty flower. There was just enough silvery light to make out the dunes of Assateague Island across the inlet. Black as sable, the sea churned and rushed inland through the narrow channel on its way to high tide.

"Speaking of Mexico..."

She smiled when his voice broke the silence; she really liked the deep sound of it.

"...I proposed to my wife in Cancún."

Her eyebrows arched before she could wrangle the reaction under control. Then immediately, her face contorted into a slight moue as she looked up at him.

He smiled softly. "You're thinking about our New Year's Eve kiss aren't you?"

"I was, actually." No matter how hard she tried,

she couldn't erase the frown that knitted her brow together.

He'd been so sweet to her that night, kissing her after she'd complained of being a fifth wheel and whined about being the only one who'd missed out on the cherished midnight tradition. Of course, it *had* been just a kiss. A charming act meant to lift her spirits. And it had done just that.

But if he was a married man... Well, that would change everything. That would make her terribly uncomfortable. It would demonstrate something unsavory about his character, wouldn't it?

"No need to worry," he promised her, shaking his head for emphasis. "Honestly."

His claim was genuine and straightforward, and it put her at ease.

During her years of running her business, she'd learned there were all types of people. Some liked to tell every little detail about their lives during their short stay. On the other end of the spectrum were those who coveted their privacy as though it were sacred. Heather always went with the flow. If her guests wanted to rage about their bosses or wax poetic about their genius grandchildren, she would listen and reply with the appropriate interjections.

And if, on the other hand, people wanted to keep to themselves and avoid interaction, she was astute enough to realize their wishes and respect them.

Until this evening, she had definitely pegged Daniel as being part of the latter group. Yes, he'd mentioned the trouble he was experiencing with his little girl, but only briefly and in the vaguest sense. Heather was sure he'd done so only because he'd felt the need to defend himself against her and Sara and Cathy's gossiping in the alley. He hadn't spoken of it again.

Because she was uncertain as to why he'd suddenly start revealing facts about himself and equally as uncertain about how she should respond or even *if* he might want her to, she simply kept quiet and waited.

"Cila and I had been dating a few years," he said. "I... I'm ashamed to admit that I put off asking her to marry me for months because several of my friends suggested she was only after a green card."

From the expectation she read in his gaze, Heather could tell he was waiting for her to reply. Finally, she said, "We put a lot of stock in the opinions of our friends."

His mouth twisted wryly and he nodded in agreement.

Daniel looked out over the swiftly flowing water. "Cila was from Burgovnia."

His use of the word '*was*' woke her up like a quick smack on the cheek.

"I knew she couldn't have been after my money," he said, a small smile massaging his tone. "I didn't have any back then. I'd only published one novel and a handful of magazine articles. I hadn't won any literary prizes yet or wowed many publishers. The fancy awards, cushy advances, the movie deals, those would come later. Much later."

The moonlight highlighted the bridge of his nose and his cheekbones with a lustrous glow. His memories made his eyes crinkle with humor one moment and his jaw muscles coil with tension the next.

"She passed away two years ago." He made the statement matter-of-factly. "She'd flown over to visit her family. I stayed here to write." He added a gruff, "Damned deadlines." Then he huffed out a sigh. "It was a simple cut that killed her. She'd fallen. Cut her arm and needed stitches. She contracted some sort of infection that got into her blood."

His throat convulsed with a swallow. "She had a raging fever that couldn't be stopped. The antibiotics seemed useless. She was gone before I could get to her. It was a very dark time in my life."

He swiveled his head, and suddenly his black-as-night eyes were boring into hers. Heather's heart ached for him, for his loss, his grief. It was carved in the lines around his mouth.

"I'm sorry." The whispered words seemed somehow insubstantial, not nearly hefty enough to convey her feelings.

Daniel continued to study her face. Finally, he said, "You're wondering why I'm pouring my heart out here."

She shook her head hard enough for her bangs to fall into her eyes. She reached up and brushed them aside. "No. I'm not."

A small smile spread across his lips. "Don't ever try to keep secrets, Heather. You're not very good at it."

Defensiveness straightened her spine, but only for a split second. Who was she kidding? She might as well be honest. The man was right. She *was* wondering. And furtiveness *wasn't* her strongest trait. She grinned and cocked her head a fraction.

"You got me," she admitted. "On both counts."

He smiled and their gazes held for a long moment... longer than what seemed appropriate. With any other man, she was certain she would have quickly become uncomfortable. But for some reason, she didn't feel that way with Daniel.

"We should probably head back, don't you think?"

She nodded in answer to his question, and they skirted around the rows of benches and started back north.

"I'll grant you this much," he said. "I don't talk about Cila very often—all of that is still pretty raw. Even after all this time. But I do have an ulterior motive."

The admission had her eyes widening. "Yes? Go on."

He was a handsome man; even more so when he smiled.

"Something's been bothering me all evening," he told her. "I want to ask you about it. But... it's going to sound very... It *is* very personal."

Her brows lifted. "O-kaaaay." Sudden suspicion stretched out the word like warm, sticky salt water taffy.

They walked a dozen yards or so in silence, and then he asked, "Are you warm enough? Would you like my coat? My gloves?"

"I'm fine, Daniel. What is it you want to know?"

He pressed his palms together and tapped both index fingers lightly against his chin. Heather could tell he was doing some deep contemplating. Finally, he exhaled forcefully.

"There's really no easy way to ask this."

She fretted, wondering just how personal this question was going to get.

"When I told you I wanted some company this evening," he began, "why did you automatically exclude yourself from the equation?"

"I excluded myself?"

"That's exactly what you did. Maybe it wasn't purposeful," he rushed to add. "But after we sorted out the initial... um, misunderstanding, and you figured out I was looking for a dinner date, you completely bypassed yourself and suggested calling Cathy."

The air temperature might have called for down

coats and fleece-lined gloves, woolen hats and scarves, but in that instant, Heather could have been in a hot, tropical climate. Her whole body broke out in anxious perspiration.

She hadn't realized what she'd done until just this moment when he'd pointed it out. Her behavior had been completely extemporaneous. He was right. During their conversation when he'd requested a date, she really had circumvented herself, and she'd done it so effortlessly, so unwittingly, it was clearly habit for her. Utterly customary behavior.

When had she become so self-oblivious?

Her heart began to pound behind her ribs and she felt a little short of breath. She unzipped her jacket a few inches and loosened her scarf, thankful when the frigid air struck her neck and chest.

"Here, let's sit down for a minute." Daniel grasped her upper arm and steered her toward a nearby bench.

Once she was seated, he settled himself beside her, twisting his body so that they were face to face, and he took one of her hands in his.

"I didn't mean to upset you."

His words were sincere, his gaze intense, but Heather brought her free hand to her face and pressed the pads of her fingers to her forehead, unable to look him in the eyes.

"You see, in my line of work," he continued, "I'm absolutely obsessed with the whys behind what people do. Why would someone go down into a basement, alone, in the dark? Why would someone quit a perfectly good job when doing so would mean being evicted and becoming homeless?"

His next question was asked so softly, the words were barely a whisper.

"Why, when a man shows interest in a woman, would she automatically offer up her friend?"

Why, indeed? The tiny question reverberated in her mind. She pressed her lips together in a thin line, knowing she couldn't avoid looking at him much longer.

When she didn't immediately respond, he said, "My gut is telling me you've shut yourself off. You've done it so thoroughly and completely that you're not even aware of what you're doing. And I'm dying to know why you'd do such a thing. What's the reason?" He lifted his hand, palm up. "For example, maybe your father abandoned your family, leaving you with self-esteem issues. Or maybe your mother is struggling with aging, and jealous of your youth, she's given you some sort of complex. Or at sometime in your past, a man has broken your heart and crushed your spirit."

She sat listening to him offer up the possibilities as though he were lobbing little balloons filled with paint meant to go splat when he hit his mark. Well, his last guess struck too close. Heather straightened up and looked at him.

"Daniel, I am not a character in one of your books."

The reply came out sounding as if it had been snipped by a sharp pair of scissors, and she wasn't surprised to see him wince.

He pulled away from her several inches. "I-I didn't," he stammered. "I mean, I wasn't..."

He paused long enough to lick his lips, and there was something about the set of his jaw that told her he'd decided against backing down.

After a slow inhalation, he said, "Real or fictionalized, Heather, it makes no difference, really. People do what they do for a reason."

Oh, she had plenty of reasons. She simply wanted to avoid discussing them with Daniel.

"Wait," she said, her eyes narrowing. "Back up a minute. What was that crazy implication you just made? '*When a man shows interest in a woman.*' What kind of fiction are you whipping up with *that*? I thought tonight was about you needing a diversion. That's what you said, remember."

"Well—" His mouth spread into a slow, sexy grin. "Having a diversion *was* my initial excuse for asking you out." Then he sobered. "But what's so crazy about me being interested in you?"

She arched a brow at him. "I think there are way too many questions being fired off around here. From both of us."

He chuckled, and the rich sound of it sent shivers coursing across her skin. Underneath her scarf, she was sure the hair on the back of her neck was standing on end.

Heather glanced up the expanse of the boardwalk but didn't see another person in sight. The pole lights made illuminated soft blue white circles on the planks.

Daniel's fingers were gentle when he captured her chin and guided her gaze to his. He must have removed his glove at some point because his bare skin was warm against her face.

He searched her gaze, studied her features for a long moment.

"I shared my experience with Cila," he said, "hoping I might smooth the way for you. Make you feel more comfortable about opening up. But if you'd rather not—"

"Why? So you can put me in one of your books?"

He shook his head, lowered his hand from her jaw. Then he shrugged one shoulder. "Because I'm curious? Because you've taken such good care of me for all these weeks? Because I'd like to get to know you? Because you're a beautiful woman and I'm—"

"Okay." She lifted her hand and swiped it through the small space between them. "You can stop now. The boloney bin is full."

His mouth compressed. "What did I say that was so unbelievable? I *am* curious. You *have* taken good care of me. I really *would* like to—" He stopped short. "Damn it, Heather. You don't think you're beautiful."

She looked out into the darkness because his expression was just too intense for her to bear.

"Look, I realize I'm not hideous or anything,

okay?" She darted a glance at his face, then focused on her lap. "Babies don't cry when I walk into a room. Children don't run screaming into the night." She offered a light laugh, but it had a hollow ring. "But let's not fool ourselves here, Daniel. Beautiful is not a word that describes me. What I mean is, I'm no supermodel." Then she muttered, "Not unless we're using a completely different definition of the word *super*."

The creases in his forehead deepened. "You don't mean that."

Just when she was about to assure him that she did, he slid his hand along her jaw line until his fingertips curled lightly around the back of her neck. Her breath caught in her throat; his fingers nestled between scarf and skin, melting every vestige of argument in her. His searching gaze roved from her eyes, to her hair, to her cheeks and nose, finally landing on her mouth.

The winter night enveloped them like chilled silk. Waves crashed against the shore in the distance, and their breath met, mingled, condensing for a moment into thin, silvery lace before rising and disappearing.

"You are the most beautiful woman I have ever seen."

He leaned toward her as he whispered the words, rounding out each one, filling it with mesmerizing significance. She became lost in his voice, lost in the moment, lost in his dark eyes.

"I've been thinking about those New Year's Eve kisses," he admitted, moving even closer. "I've been wondering about the taste of your lips, the scent of your skin."

His fingers slid a bit deeper and with slightest pressure, he pulled her toward him.

He intended to kiss her. That much was unmistakable. And in that instant, she wanted nothing more.

CHAPTER FIVE

He placed a kiss, light and sweet, on the corner of her mouth. Her eyelids fluttered closed as anticipation churned in the pit of her belly like an eddying tide, but the moment was over almost before it began. She immediately sensed he leaned away from her, and when she looked at him, she saw him staring at her, his heavy-lidded gaze filled with...

Warning bells went off in her head, nerve-jarringly loud; however, she blocked them out, shoved them as far to the back of her brain as she could in order to snuff them out like a just-lit match.

It had been so long since she'd felt desired. So long since she'd felt wanted. Savoring this rare sensation, if only for a few fleeting minutes, became the most important thing in her existence.

His mouth slanted down across hers, hot and moist. Her heart pounded and her breath quickened. Something akin to electricity skittered throughout her body, sparking to life from somewhere near her diaphragm and emanating outward, coursing down her arms and legs, setting fire to her nerve endings.

The cold, salty air mingled with the warm-leather scent of his skin, a contrast that would surely leave its mark on her memory for the rest of her life. His lips were soft yet firm, a paradoxical combination that swept every thought from her head; all she knew was that she didn't want this experience to end. Ever.

Daniel deepened the kiss, and she parted her lips for him. She savored the faint sweetness of caramel and earthy hops from the beer he'd enjoyed with dinner. The urge to lean into him was strong, and far off, she heard a soft, sexy susurrus, a sound somewhere between a mew and a purr, that clearly expressed pleasure. Through the fog of her thoughts, she realized the noises were coming from her, and the desire pulsing inside her burgeoned.

His kiss sparked a flame in her belly, way down deep and visceral, and the light friction of his fingertips gliding over her jaw and down her neck fueled the fire. It was heightened further by the feathery bristle of his five o'clock shadow against her chin. Her breathing turned shallow and rapid; his sounded labored, as well. Every touch, every taste, every sound magnified the greedy hunger that rumbled and growled its way to life.

"Your cheeks are ice cold," he whispered the words against her mouth.

"I'm fine." She wasn't sure if she'd actually voiced the words or merely thought them.

How could her skin feel cold to him when she felt sure she was burning up inside?

"We should get back before you freeze."

No. This time, she knew her reaction was only a thought. She didn't want the kiss to end. She wanted to feel his hands on her skin, his lips on hers.

But she felt hazy, drugged, as if she'd consumed straight shots of tequila earlier rather than a small glass of wine. Daniel's kiss was inebriating, and a soft, vague smile settled on her lips as she reveled in the fuzzy feeling he'd caused.

He pulled her to her feet, tucked her hand in the crook of his arm. Laying her head against his shoulder seemed like the most natural thing in the world to do as they made their way toward The Lonely Loon.

He made an attempt at conversation, completely one-sided, complimenting the quaintness of Ocean City, and commenting on how large the town felt, empty of tourists. He talked of other tourist destinations he'd visited during the off-season.

Heather remained silent, listening to the low, entrancing sound of his rumbling voice, happily snuggled in the cozy bubble enveloping her. But all too soon they reached home. They climbed the steps to the front porch and she unlocked the front door.

After shucking off his coat, he helped her out of hers, hanging them both on the ornate wooden hooks on the wall of the foyer. He turned around unexpectedly and wrapped his arms around her.

"Thank you, Heather." He kissed her forehead. "Tonight was just what I needed to clear my mind." He heaved a sigh. "You forced me to focus on something else for a while. I'm grateful."

"The book is giving you problems?"

"The book." His sexy mouth leveled for a brief moment, then he added, "And other things."

The despair that suddenly tinged his tone concerned her. He must be pining for his little girl. But before she could ask him anything more, he pulled her tight against his chest.

Being this close to another human being—a man—felt alien to her; it had been that long since she'd been hugged, kissed, touched. She wanted to slip her arms around his neck, rove her hands across his broad back. She imagined his muscles, hard and corded, beneath her fingertips. But she didn't move. Couldn't act.

"Can I kiss you goodnight?" he asked.

However, the shyness that made her hesitant wasn't strong enough to keep her from murmuring, "I'd be disappointed if you didn't."

He kissed her then, intensely, thoroughly, and

that drunken feeling made her deliciously dizzy. It was as if the muscles in her legs slowly slid down her bones, and when he pulled away from her, she feared her wobbly knees wouldn't hold her weight.

"So you never answered my question." He smoothed his palms over her shoulders, settling his hands lightly on her upper arms. "Who broke your heart, Heather? Who made you start thinking of yourself as less than the gorgeous woman you are?"

She didn't immediately reply because she needed time to sort out her thoughts. Her knee-jerk reaction was to dismiss his compliment and leave it at that. No one in their right mind would think she was gorgeous, and his use of the word was purely to make her feel good, she was sure. But making any type of fuss about it would only give him evidence to bend and twist to prove his point.

Their impromptu dinner date had been wonderful. He'd made her feel interesting, pretty even. The kisses they'd shared had been intimate, sweet, and excruciatingly enjoyable. His close proximity, the warm scent of him, the manner in which he focused solely on her, the memory of his lips lingering on hers, his whispered compliments, the desire that had glittered in his gaze, all continued to intoxicate her.

The fact that she had instinctively mistaken his dinner invitation as something completely different than what it had been was a startling revelation for her, and his curiosity about it was understandable. But revealing what happened to her in the past, her experience with rejection, hurt, and anger, would only spoil all the good things they'd shared tonight. She refused to mar what was sure to become a perfect memory for her by revealing her ugly story.

"I hate to disappoint you," she told him, "but my life's been fairly normal. A balance of happiness and heartache." She smiled. "Just like everyone else."

What she'd told him wasn't a lie.

She splayed the flat of her palm on his chest, relishing the heat of his skin beneath the soft cotton. It wasn't like her to be so bold, but the kisses they'd shared made her surprisingly fearless.

"Although I never knew my biological father," she continued, "I had lots of father-figures. Friends of my mom's who loved me like a daughter. I still keep in contact with many of them. We exchange

Christmas cards, birthday cards, that kind of thing."

Her smile went a tad crooked. "And if you'd had the opportunity to meet my mother, you'd understand there wasn't a jealous bone in her body. Every single one of her bones was made of pure, unadulterated confidence." Heather chuckled. "She used to brag about having been proposed to over a dozen times, by a dozen different men. She'd have never struggled with growing old. She'd have partied her way through it." Heather pursed her lips, and then she added, "Mom didn't get the chance, though. She passed away years ago."

Daniel's handsome face contorted with sympathy and he murmured condolences. She slid her hand a few inches up his pectoral muscles in response. Her fingertips nestled against his collarbone.

Vaguely, she was aware of a citrusy scent that mingled with the warm leather she'd already taken note of. She would have loved nothing more than leaning into him, pressing her nose to his neck, closing her eyes, and inhaling. Gently pushing the errant thought from her mind, she said, "And although I was in a serious relationship in the past, my spirit is anything but crushed."

She placed her other hand on his chest, and gazed up at him through lowered lashes. "So that leaves us with no daddy issues. No mommy issues. And plenty of sassy attitude."

To prove her point, she lifted herself up onto her toes and kissed him squarely on the mouth.

"Thank you for the lovely evening."

He kissed her back, clearly communicating his ravenous yearning, and Heather's heart fluttered like moth's wings. But wanting desperately to end their "date" on a high note, she stepped away from him and turned toward the stairs.

She'd climbed four steps when she heard him say, "I'm sorry my assumptions were so far off the mark."

Heather paused, holding the banister, and twisting her upper body just enough that she could look into his face. "No harm done. You can't get it right every time."

Then she returned to her saunter, knowing his eyes were glued to her rear.

~*~

She'd barely closed her bedroom door before she was reaching for her phone and creating a group text.

Heather: You. Will. Not. Believe. This.

Sara: You okay?

Cathy: What trouble did you get into now?

Heather: I went on a date.

Cathy: WHAT?

Cathy: When? Tonight?

Cathy: With who?

Sara: Shouldn't that be with whom?

Cathy: Bite me, Sara. With who, Heather? Who? Who?

Sara: Slow down, Miz Owl. Your thumbs are going to explode.

Cathy: I need answers

Cathy: !!!!!

Heather typed out a reply to Cathy's first question only because she'd already begun thumbing in the response about when.

Heather: Yes, tonight. Unplanned, of course. But very fun.

Cathy: Who?

Sara: Who?

Cathy: WHO?

The only reason she hesitated was because she knew Cathy didn't think much of Daniel. What Heather saw as the quirks of an introverted, creative personality, Cathy claimed were anti-social, standoffish, and even self-centered traits.

Cathy: Heather needs to type faster.

Sara: lol Now that's something I can agree with.

Cathy: Heather on a date? *swoon, thud*

Heather: Not surprised by your reaction. I nearly fainted myself.

Cathy: Do you think she passed out?

Cathy: Is she ever going to tell us who?

Cathy: Heather! Don't make me come over there.

Heather bit her lip, straightened her spine, and thumbed in the letters.

Heather: Daniel

For ten long seconds, the screen of her phone showed no new texts. She let out a soft, dismal groan.

"Heather, you idiot," she whispered to the empty room. "They think you've made a huge mistake."

Heather: It started out as a distraction.
Heather: For him.
Heather: To get away from his work.
Heather: Probably wasn't really a date at all.

With each entry, her shoulders rounded a little more. She deeply respected the opinions of her friends. And although it was rare that they disapproved of something she said or did, if they expressed the least amount of criticism, Heather was always quick to rethink her words and actions.

Finally, a message popped up.

Sara: Did you have a good time?
Heather: So SO good.
Cathy: So-so?

Heather: No dash. SO GOOD!
Sara: Woot!

Heather smiled, reading Sara's exclamation. If worse came to worst, a fifty percent approval rating would be good enough for her. She chuckled out loud and realized she was relieved. The thoughts and feelings of these two women really mattered. A lot.

Cathy: He's leaving soon.
Sara: Don't be a party pooper, Cath.
Cathy: Just sayin'.
Heather: Point taken. It was only a kiss. Well...

Remembering the way Daniel's lips nearly devoured hers, she grinned wickedly, and her heart skipped behind her ribs.

Sara: Well, what?
Heather: Several kisses, actually. Several HOT kisses.
Cathy: Calm down a second. He's moody. He's guarded. He's

Cathy: Sorry. Typing too fast. He's not very approachable. I don't see him as your type.

Heather threw her head back and laughed.

Heather: I've got a type?
Sara: Let's not pick the man apart. It's a holiday fling.

Back when the girls were in their teens, they'd enjoyed their fair share of holiday romances, a weekend or a week, sometimes two, of dating boys whose families were vacationing at the beach. These meaningless relationships were called by several risqué names—summer romances, seven-day rendezvous, weekend affairs—not because anything lewd ever happened, of course, but more because the suggestive monikers made the girls feel more mature. More adult than they actually were. The summer flings were always innocent, at least where Heather was concerned anyway. She had slept with one man and one man only in her whole life, and he had stomped on her heart like it was a detestable stink bug.

Although, she couldn't really blame Steve for

what had happened between them. She'd done what she'd done and there had been no turning back.

Cathy: Ah. Okay. I get it. A romp in the salt marsh. Might be just what you need.

Heather: No romping. Just a bit of kissing. And flirting.

Cathy: And what do you think kissing and flirting lead to?

Sara: Heather, hon, maybe it's time to open your heart.

Cathy: What she needs to do is open her knees.

The mere thought of making love with Daniel conjured the wildest array of reactions in her. Her body flushed with heat, but an icy anxiety trickled through her veins as well. To want something but not want it felt crazy. Peculiar. Odder than odd.

Cathy: Don't mind me. Feeling a bit off kilter.

Sara: Horny, more like.

Heather: lol

Cathy: Bradley canceled our date again tonight.

Second cancellation since he returned home from visiting his parents.

Sara: So what's going on?

Cathy: No clue. He's acting weird. Aloof. Strange word, but it fits.

Cathy: Sorry for whining.

Heather: Think he's met someone?

Heather's thumbs hovered over the keypad, but she didn't type out "again."

If someone were to write a book about Cathy and Bradley's relationship an apt title would be On Again, Off Again, or The Bed Buddy Battle.

Cathy: Sorry for being a downer.

Cathy: Heather, have some fun with Daniel.

Cathy: Just don't get serious. I don't trust the man.

Heather: Don't worry. As fun as it was, it was a one-time thing, I'm sure.

But even as she typed out the words, Heather hoped she was wrong. She'd enjoyed Daniel's kisses way too much not to experience a few more before he left Ocean City for good.

Sara: Cathy, you don't trust ANY man.

Cathy: Oh, I don't know. Landon's pretty cool.

Sara: You're just saying that because he installed a water shut off valve in the café.

Cathy: *grin* Like I said, he's pretty cool.

Heather: Hey, speaking of Landon... Did you tell him? Did you pee on that stick? Can you tell us yet?

Cathy: Put us out of our misery already. Are we going to be aunties?

Heather: What did Landon say?

Sara: Intended to tell you both face to face tomorrow, but since you asked...

Sara: Yes. Yes. Yes. Yes. And Landon is ecstatic!

Heather: OMG

Cathy: *speechless*

Sara: Well, that's a first for you. Somebody make a note!

Heather: Congrats. So happy for you, sweetie. Can't wait to shop for the baby!

Sara: He wants to get married. Squeee!

Cathy: Whoa. I'm happy about the baby. But being preggo is no reason to get shackled.

Sara: Cathy. Shut up. I love the man.

Cathy: Whatever.

CHAPTER SIX

At breakfast the following morning, Heather stood in the doorway of the dining room, studying Daniel as she inadvertently worried a striped tea towel between her fingers. He sat at the table, hunched over a yellow legal pad filled with penciled notes. Every once in a while he would check off an item or add a another thought to the long list.

She hated to bother him, but it was nearly ten o'clock and he'd been sitting there for over an hour.

When she'd placed the food on the sideboard, he hadn't looked up, hadn't made a move to fill his plate. He hadn't even noticed when she'd refreshed his cup of coffee.

There had been mornings in the past when work had engulfed him to the point that he hadn't eaten until the food had gone stone cold. She'd made buttermilk pancakes, sausage patties, and fresh cinnamon-laced applesauce this morning. Pancakes were always best eaten while they were still hot and moist and fluffy, dripping with melted butter and maple syrup. And if those little sausage patties were allowed to grow cold, they'd turn into miniature hockey pucks. Yes, the hot food was sitting on an electric warming tray, but every cook worth her while knew it would dry out eventually despite the most valiant efforts.

Heather resisted the urge to pace. She didn't know what was wrong with her. It wasn't as if her guests couldn't skip breakfast if they chose to do so. He was a grown man. If he wanted to work rather than eat that's exactly what he should do. But when he did eventually eat, and surely he would, wouldn't the stale pancakes and hard sausage rounds be a reflection on her?

Tucking the towel into the waistband of her apron, she had every intention of going into the kitchen and leaving him to work in peace. But she took one step and then another, not toward the kitchen, but toward the sideboard.

She served up three pancakes, slathered them with butter, drizzled them with syrup, and then placed three patties of sausage on the plate. She practically tip-toed across the floor, and then she set the food near the spot where his forearm rested on the corner of the tabletop. Just as she turned, his fingers lightly encircled her wrist, stopping her forward motion.

"Thank you, Heather," he said.

His tone was warm and low, and it sent shivers up her spine.

She turned and looked into his face, smiling. "You're welcome."

"I love pancakes."

"I know you do," she told him. "I've noticed that you eat a little more breakfast when I serve pancakes."

His thumb roved lazily across the back of her hand, making her feel all breathless and raising a stark vision in her mind of how utterly incredible it felt when he'd touched her cheek, her neck, her shoulder, kissed her mouth last night.

"I'm sorry that I'm preoccupied this morning." His coal black gaze darted to the pad of paper and then back up to her face. "A scene came to me this morning and I really must get it down before I lose something."

"That's all right. I completely understand." Heather reached out and slid the plate an inch closer to him. "But could you eat while you work? I'll worry all day, otherwise. I really don't like it when you skip breakfast, because very often I can hear you tapping on your keyboard right through lunch. That can't be healthy."

The corners of his mouth turned up, and for a second or two, she couldn't take her attention off his face. With those big, dark eyes, that thick wavy hair, and those sharp cheekbones, he would make gorgeous babies.

The unexpected thought made Heather's eyes go wide and her smile slipped. Why would she think such a thing?

Ah, yes. Of course. It was Sara's news from last night that induced the baby-making thought.

Heather let her eyelids slide closed for a moment as she took a deep, collective breath.

"I will eat."

She looked at him when he spoke and smiled at the humor etched around his mouth.

"And I thank you for worrying about me."

Heather blinked. "W-well, I worry about all my guests."

Her momentary stammer caused his expression to shift just the slightest bit; his facial muscles softened with a... *knowing*. And as they stared into each other's eyes, she felt as if he perceived her every thought, recognized that her concern for him had grown overnight into something important, something much more profound than it had been only days before.

Softly, he said, "I know you do."

The breath in her throat caught and held, and when his gaze latched onto her mouth, her pulse went haywire. The very molecules of air seemed to swell until they were engorged with—

Her phone trilled, alerting her to a text message, and she felt as if a magician had snapped his fingers and awakened her from a heavy trance. After offering him a self-conscious smile, she stepped away, and slipped her hand into her pocket to retrieve her cell phone.

She chuckled lightly at Sara's text, grateful to have escaped the sultry longing that had charged the small space between her and Daniel.

"Sara's baked a new cookie recipe," she told him. "She wants Cathy and me to meet her in the foyer for a sample. Want to take a break? Her cookies are always delicious."

"I appreciate the offer, but I really do need to get to work." He slid his chair out and picked up his legal pad. "I have to get this into the computer. Before I forget something."

"Of course." She nodded. "It's okay. But you will eat, won't you?"

His eyes crinkled and he reached out and gave her shoulder a gentle squeeze. "I will. I promise. I'll take the plate up with me."

The loud knock on the front door caused Heather to frown as she swiveled her head toward the sound.

"Hmmm. I wonder who that could be. Cathy and Sara never knock." She turned back to him and waved her hands as if to shoo him upstairs.

"Go on. Get to work. I'll see that you're not disturbed."

She hurried through the dining room and into the foyer to open the door.

The young woman standing on the porch looked to be in her late twenties. Her blonde hair was pulled up into one of those floppy, messy buns that was the going style these days, and her blue eyes flashed as brightly as her smile.

"Hi," she said. "Are you the owner?"

Heather nodded, but before she could say anything, the girl continued to talk.

"I was walking out front and saw this beautiful building. I'd love to do a story on your B&B. The Lonely Loon. I love that name. I'd love to hear the history of the building, how you got started, local attractions and restaurants, and what not." Her smile widened. "And you, too, of course. I'd certainly include you in the story."

The blonde's enthusiasm and her soft, southern twang made Heather smile. "A story for what? A magazine? A newspaper?" She lifted both hands, palms up.

"Oh, I'm sorry. My name is Sandra Douglas." She fumbled around in her enormous leather purse and pulled out a business card. "I work for Atlantic Coastal magazine."

"Atlantic Coastal? But you're based in Georgia, right?" Heather liked the idea of the story. It would give her a little publicity. "Aren't you a little far north?"

The questions made the journalist's eyes widen slightly. "W-well, you are on the Atlantic coast."

Heather chuckled. "You're right about that."

"Oh, I'm sorry." Sandra shifted her bag higher on her shoulder. "I don't normally make cold calls like this. But I just... happened to pass by."

A curious awkwardness swiftly filled the next second or two of silence, a telling sign to Heather that Sandra was out of her element. She reached out her hand and smiled in an attempt to ease the young woman's anxiety.

"I'm Heather Phillips. I own The Loon and I'd love to see my B&B in Atlantic Coastal. That would be wonderful."

Sandra's body visibly relaxed. "That's great. My boss will be pleased." Her gaze darted beyond Heather into the inner confines of the house. "Could I come in and look around?"

"Actually, you can't," Heather told her. "Today's

not a good day for you to take a tour. I have a guest who needs the house to be quiet. He's working and I don't want to disturb him. Won't you need a photographer, anyway?"

"Oh, yeah." Her brow furrowed. "I do have a camera, but I left it in my hotel room." She let out a short bark of laughter. "Silly of me, huh? As I said, I was just passing by."

"How about this idea," Heather said. "We can go downstairs to the café and I'll answer any questions you have. Then this evening or tomorrow, when we've figured out a time that will work, you can come back to look around The Loon and take your pictures."

The young woman took a small step backwards. "Well, I-I, um, really don't have time right now. But, um, could you meet me for coffee? Tomorrow? Mid-morning? At the Starbucks in West Ocean City? I'm staying in a hotel over there."

Heather unwittingly lifted her hand, resting it on her hip. The reporter's sudden withdrawal took her aback. One minute she wanted a tour, the next minute she didn't have time to ask her questions. Heather tried to go with the flow, doing her best to hide her bewilderment.

"Sure, um..." She nodded vaguely. "I can do that."

"That's great. Thank you." Sandra smiled as she hitched her purse up onto her shoulder again. "I'll see you around ten in the morning, then?"

"That sounds perfect. I'll be there." Heather hoped her smile was wide enough to defeat the frown that kept trying to force itself onto her brow.

Just seconds later, Sandra had descended the front stairs and was hurrying along the boardwalk.

While Heather was still standing at the door, Sara came up the steps, a plate balanced in one hand. And then Cathy followed close on her heels.

"What's up?" Sara asked. "You look like you've seen a bona fide merman."

"Yeah, you look flummoxed," Cathy added.

Sara looked askance at Cathy, laughing. "*Flummoxed?*"

"Dictionary.com's Word of the Day." Cathy grinned. "I'm a subscriber." Then Cathy asked Heather, "What's the matter with you?"

Heather offered a vague shrug and pointed toward the reporter who was half a block away. "That young woman wanted to do a story on The Lonely Loon, but..."

Sara and Cathy both turned to see who she was talking about.

"Hey," Cathy said, "she was just in The Grill. Had a coffee. Said she wanted to book a room. I told her there were no rooms available."

Cathy and Sara were both aware that Daniel had booked the B&B for the winter. They knew about his quest to finish his novel.

Cathy swiveled her gaze back to Heather. "Thought I'd save you the trouble of having to break the bad news to her." She reached up and pinched her chin. "Now that I think about it, when she learned there were no vacancies, she seemed a bit discombobulated."

Sara's mouth quirked up. "You're loving that Word of the Day thing, huh?"

Cathy ignored her. "She didn't say anything about doing a story, though."

"That is really strange." Heather's tone went soft. "She told me she was staying in a hotel in West Ocean City." She swiped her hands together then brushed her palms down the thighs of her trousers. "Oh, well. I'm meeting her tomorrow morning. I'll sure I'll find out what's going on there."

She smiled at Sara, then looked at the plate of cookies. "So what do we have here?"

Sara beamed with pride. "These are Vegan Oatmeal Raisin Cookies."

"*Vegan?*" Cathy's fingers had been a mere inch from the plate, but then she pulled her hand back to her chest. "Doesn't that mean—"

"No butter, no eggs, no animal products," Sara finished for her. Then she chuckled at Cathy's expression. "Oh, come on. Keep an open mind."

Heather picked up a cookie and sniffed it, the rich scent of cinnamon making her mouth water.

"I had two different customers request a vegan cookie to give as gifts this past Christmas," Sara told them. "I had nothing to offer them. So I've been experimenting."

Heather took a bite, and she was surprised by how flavorful the cookie tasted. "It's light. And moist. Love the cinnamon." She chewed. "The raisins offer a nice sweetness, but the cookie itself isn't overly sweet. Nice oat flavor." She savored the goodness in her mouth and then swallowed, tipping her head just a bit. "Is that walnuts I taste in there?"

Sara's smile was back. "Yes. I toasted them for

this batch, and then ground them up in the food processor. Good?"

"They're delicious," Cathy exclaimed, reaching for another and taking a big bite. "I always imagined vegan recipes tasting like cardboard."

"Well, then," Sara quipped, "I'm so glad you're wrong. Again."

Cathy screwed up her face in response.

"Who wants a cup of tea?" Heather took a small, backward step toward the front door. "Water's already hot. I just need to pass out teabags and pour."

"But isn't the bestseller writing?" Cathy asked.

Heather turned and waved them inside. "He is, but we'll be okay if we stay in the kitchen."

"And we whisper," Sara teased, following Heather.

"And tiptoe across these wood floors." Cathy's loud whisper made Sara snicker and Cathy quickly joined in.

Heather only offered them a long-suffering sigh. They might try to annoy the hell out of her far too often, but she wouldn't trade them, not even for a truckload of gold bars.

~*~

Heather pushed her way into the Starbucks, not surprised that there was a line at the counter. As she stood waiting for her turn to order, she saw Sandra sitting at a nearby table near the front window, her focus on her open laptop.

The chilly January day called for the rich, warm spiciness of a chai latte, and once Heather had the drink in hand, she weaved around the tables and chairs as she made her way over to the reporter.

"Hey, there, Sandra," she greeted. "How are you today?"

The young woman smiled, but Heather could tell there was edginess about her.

"Hi," she said. "I'm good. How about you?"

"I'm great." Heather slid out a chair and sat down. "Before you start asking me any questions, I need to be upfront with you about a few things. I called the magazine this morning."

Sandra looked surprised.

"The woman I spoke with told me you do work for the Atlantic Coastal."

The cell phone that sat on the table began to vibrate, but Sandra didn't reach for it.

"But she seemed unaware of any Ocean City assignment," Heather continued.

Sandra sat up straighter, then opened her mouth to speak, but Heather cut her off.

"I also want you to know that my friend owns The Sunshine Grill downstairs from The Loon." She laced her fingers around the cup of warm chai. "She told me that you had asked her if there any vacancies at my B&B, and that she told you—"

"I never said I was on assignment," Sandra blurted. "I told you I was walking by. It was a whim, really. I thought your B&B would make a nice story. But if you'd rather not be in the magazine, if you'd rather not get all that great coverage, that's fine by me."

She ended her huff by slamming shut her laptop.

Heather wasn't the least bit ruffled. And she didn't fail to notice that the woman seemed to find it impossible to meet her gaze.

"I learned one other thing from making the call," Heather said. "You're not a writer, Sandra. You're an editor. Of advertising copy."

At that moment, Sandra's cell phone began to vibrate again. She picked it up, glanced at the caller ID, turned off the ringer, and set it aside.

"Well, that was kind of her," she muttered. "I'm not actually an editor. I'm a proofer. I stare at advertisements all day long, looking for typos." She finally lifted deadpan eyes to meet Heather's as she added, "It's such a *glamorous* job, let me tell you."

Heather set her cup down on the tabletop. "I have to say, you're not very good at subterfuge. And you don't think all that fast on your feet. The way you balked after I suggested we go downstairs to The Grill to talk. Your behavior set my suspicions tingling. And it wasn't very smart to tell Cathy one thing and tell me another."

Sandra rolled her eyes. "How could I know you two knew each other?"

"We work in the same building," Heather gently pointed out.

It wasn't Heather's aim to embarrass the girl; she just wanted to cut through the lies to get to the truth as quickly as possible.

"Listen, hon." Heather leaned forward. "Why don't you tell me what this is all about?"

She smiled, but she had to admit, after speaking with the woman at Atlantic Coastal this morning, she'd felt completely stumped. Why in the world would this girl approach her like she had? Why would she lie?

"I'm tired of proofing," Sandra finally said. "And I don't want to be an editor. I want to be a *writer*. And paying writing gigs are few and far between in this business. Newspapers are shutting down. Everyone is going digital. It's... it's hard."

Heather gently pried the plastic lid off her tea. She lifted the rim to her mouth and took a sip. The heady tastes hit her tongue: cardamom, nutmeg, ginger, and cloves, and the richly scented steam wafted around her face.

The answer Sandra gave was completely plausible. It seemed like a perfectly natural thing for a journalist wannabe to do... write an interesting story about The Lonely Loon and present it to the magazine's publisher as proof of her writing skills.

Heather nodded. "I see." She set the cup down again, pleased by the calm demeanor that she'd been able to present. As she'd driven over to the west side of town, she'd fretted about the confrontation. But it had been simple, really. Just asking for the simple truth had been the best solution.

There were still a couple of questions niggling at her, though. "But why lie?" she asked. "Why didn't you just tell me you were going after a writing job at your magazine?"

Sandra's chin tipped up, and she unwittingly slid her palm over the silver laptop that sat on the table, her gaze zeroing in on Heather's face. "You would have helped me get a story?"

"Of course, I would help you." Heather smiled. "I like to see people succeed. If I can help you, I will." *You silly twit*, whispered through her mind, but luckily she was able to keep the offensive moniker from slipping off her tongue. "Who wouldn't like to help someone advance in their career?"

"Oh, wow," Sandra gushed. "I don't know what to say. I just... this is so nice of you."

Heather's smile widened. Now that the truth was sitting like an open book in front of them, they could get down to work. She could tell Sandra that her mother had been the one who had established The Lonely Loon, and she could explain where the name had come from. And how she'd taken over the business after her mother had died of breast cancer. She'd be sure to name a few of the neighboring boardwalk businesses and their owners to offer as much promotion to her friends as she could. The owners of the shops, restaurants, and hotels on the boardwalk were a tight-knit group.

Sandra reached into her satchel and pulled out an eight by ten piece of paper and slid it across the table.

"What's this?" Heather asked.

As her eyes scanned the short, full-caps header—WRITER DB ATWELL'S DAUGHTER MISSING. Heather's blood froze and she felt like she were sitting in a vacuum.

"*This* is the story I want." The words burst from Sandra like blustery wind during a nor'easter. "I have a friend who works at the Associated Press. He sent this to me just before Christmas. It's taken me weeks to track him down. DB Atwell, I mean. The teachers at his daughter's school aren't talking. His publisher isn't talking. Even his agent blew me off."

Heather watched Sandra's mouth moving, she even heard the words, but the situation had taken such a bizarre turn, that she felt truly dumbfounded.

"I've tracked him to Ocean City, I believe," Sandra continued. "And although I haven't seen him, I'm pretty sure he's hiding out at your B&B. He's the one you mentioned yesterday, isn't he? The guest who needs quiet. I want you to tell me about him. I *need* you to tell me everything you know. About him. And his missing daughter."

CHAPTER SEVEN

A thick blanket of clouds had moved in to cover the sky and a slight wind had kicked up. Heather slipped on her coat and gloves, and wrapped a scarf around her neck before setting off down the boardwalk. She'd driven straight home from her meeting with Sandra Douglas, her intention to have a serious talk with Daniel. However, she'd arrived to an empty house. Daniel's car was in its parking spot, so he must be out on foot, either walking on the boardwalk or the beach or downtown or over on the bay.

She'd tried busying herself as she waited for him, and now there was a roast in the crock pot and the dishes in the dishwasher were put away. But the antsy feeling in her stomach refused to let up, so she'd decided to go out looking for him. A crazy notion really when she had no idea where he might have gone, but she couldn't help herself.

The air was damp, bone-chilling, and Heather stuffed her hands deep into her pockets and hunkered deeper into her coat for warmth. She'd only walked half a block when she saw him trudging across the sand. How he could stay out in this weather for hours on end, she had no idea.

He spent a lot of time on the beach, and Heather figured that meant he was struggling with his story, working out the details of a particular scene or one of his characters. Heather loved to read, especially enjoying those books that swept her away, that allowed her to lose herself in a well-told tale. But she'd never taken the time to ponder how authors went about writing one. All those chapters. All those words. Like wooden blocks built, one upon the next, to create an intricate structure. In the weeks since Daniel had been at The Loon, she'd learned the process could be arduous—not in a physical sense, of course, but it was clearly mentally taxing.

But now Heather realized, the hours Daniel spent wandering the shore probably had more to do with his daughter than it had his book. What was he doing in Ocean City if his daughter was missing? Was he using The Loon as a hideaway? Was his daughter really missing? If she was, where on earth was she? And why wasn't Daniel searching for her? None of this made any sense.

She veered off through the opening in the sea wall, and took the stairs down to the sand. Her jaw clenched tighter with each step until her back teeth actually began to ache. Sandra and that snippet from AP had planted some awful questions in her head. She waved to get Daniel's attention, and as soon as he saw her, he started jogging toward her.

He wasn't wearing a hat, so the wind whipped at his hair. Even with his cheeks ruddy from the cold, he radiated the kind of attraction that made women's heads turn.

"Hey," he said, smiling.

"You're half frozen."

"I'm all right." Then he frowned. "I don't like that look on your face. What is it, Heather? What's wrong?"

She sighed and ran her tongue across her lips. The wind cut across the wet skin like an icy dagger. "I need to talk to you. Can we go back to The Loon? Have you had lunch? I'll make you a sandwich."

"How about we go to the cafe?" he offered. He rubbed his hands together. "Saves you from making a mess in your kitchen. A bowl of hot soup would warm us both up."

Before long, they were pushing their way through the door of The Sunshine Grill. The television on the wall played the afternoon news. The place was empty except for the two elderly locals talking politics over coffee at the counter.

Cathy eyed them curiously, and Heather called out their orders of tomato soup and grilled cheese sandwiches so she wouldn't have to walk across the restaurant. Daniel took off his coat and tossed it onto the bench seat, then helped Heather off with hers. Soon they were settled across from each other in the corner booth by the front window. None of the booths and tables offered complete privacy, but they would be less likely to be overheard here.

"I love this place," Heather told him. "It always feels so homey to me."

"The food's good." Daniel nodded, not taking his gaze off her face. "Although the proprietor can be a little prickly."

She knew he came to the cafe to eat quite regularly.

"So, what is it?" he asked. "I don't like that look of gloom on your face."

She tried to smile, but she knew she failed miserably.

"I just met with a reporter—or rather a person claiming to be a reporter. This morning. Over in West Ocean City," she told him. "She knocked on my front door yesterday out of the blue. Asked if she could do a story on The Loon." She paused. Then, shaking her head, she got to the point, "But it turns out she's not a reporter. And she isn't interested in The Loon at all. The story she wants is about you... and your daughter."

He was quiet for the next several minutes as she filled him in on everything she knew about Sandra, the small, regional magazine where the reporter worked, and the AP article about Daniel and his daughter.

Finally, she said, "I don't think Atlantic Coastal would be interested in the story. From what I've seen, the magazine features interviews with local business people, photo tours of historic homes in the south east, that sort of thing. The only way to get a copy this far north is if you're a subscriber. The girl is looking to turn this into something sensational. Something that might get her noticed by a big newspaper, or one of those awful gossip rags, heaven forbid. She's desperate to see her name in a byline."

The worry lines creasing his forehead had her assuring him, "I didn't tell her anything, Daniel. She wasn't even sure you were staying at The Loon. I want you to know that I'd never talk about you, or any other guest for that matter. To anyone. For any amount of money."

"She offered you money?"

"Yes." Heather grinned. "But she found out pretty quickly that that was the wrong thing to do. I told her she'd better never come within a mile of The Loon ever again or I'd call the police and file harassment charges." She chuckled. "The police would probably laugh at me, but from the look on that girl's face, she didn't know that. And then I walked out."

Gratitude brightened his coal-dark eyes and he reached across the table to cover her hand with his. Heather's heart swelled in her chest and she was relieved that he didn't seem to be too awfully upset by her news. He murmured his thanks just as Cathy began setting their lunch on the table. The soup bowl was thumped in front of Daniel with enough force to slosh some of the thick, red liquid onto the tabletop and he instinctively leaned back, pulling his arm away from Heather.

"Cathy!" Heather said, scrambling for a napkin. "Careful there."

"Sorry."

But Heather heard not an ounce of regret in her friend's tone.

Cathy emptied the tray of the sandwiches, cutlery, and glasses of water, and then offered Daniel a quick, plastic smile before turning and walking away.

He just shook his head, his mouth flattening with irony. "With all this friendly service, it's a wonder this place isn't packed to the corners with customers."

"Sorry about that," Heather said. "She's a bit protective of me."

He gazed at Cathy's retreating figure and murmured, "I can see that."

The spoon felt cool against Heather's fingers. She dipped into the soup and tasted it. Cathy's homemade soups were always delicious and this was no exception with its bits of fire-roasted tomato and the drizzle of basil oil on top.

"So..." Heather heard the tentative quality in her voice. "Tell me about your little girl. Has she really disappeared?"

He spent a lot of time fussing on his side of the table—placing the paper napkin on his lap, arranging his fork and spoon, picking up his sandwich and breaking off a piece, then taking a small bite.

She remained patient, took another swallow of soup, hoping that the quiet between them didn't last long enough to become awkward.

He lifted his gaze to hers. "Her name's Mia," he said softly.

Heather's spoon was poised in front of her lips, but she paused, listening.

"I know who she's with." Daniel placed the sandwich back on the plate. "But I don't know where she is. Exactly. And I don't mind admitting that this whole damn situation is slowly killing me."

Ever so gently, she put down the spoon. Her appetite shriveled and evaporated as if it had never existed.

She felt as though her throat was coated in sandpaper as she whispered, "I don't understand, Daniel. What do you mean?"

He sighed as he reached for his napkin. "In order to explain things, I have to go back to mid-November. Hell, that's not true. I have to go back two years... back to when my wife died in Burgovnia. Cila's family wasn't happy when I decided to bring her body back to the States for burial. I thought it would be best for Mia to have her mother's remains here. So we could take flowers to her grave. And spend time remembering. But Cila's family acted like I was doing something sacrilegious. They were very unhappy when I wasn't able to stay in Burgovnia for the full mourning period. A month is a long time for a child to be subjected to..." He heaved another sigh. "It's not that I meant to insult their beliefs. We stayed for ten days, and all Mia did was cry. She couldn't seem to sleep, and when she did, she had nightmares. Seeing all that grief just wasn't healthy for her. So I packed up our things and we flew home. Cila's father made it very clear he was disappointed in me. Jakob Brankov can be a very stern individual."

Daniel scooted his sandwich on the plate, but didn't take a bite. "Jakob brought his other daughter, Anica, to visit us here last year. They stayed a week, and I thought everything went well."

He rubbed his fingers up and down his water glass. "Jakob has been complaining for months about seeing Mia. Anica has written me a truckload of letters and she's called every week. They didn't want Mia to forget where she was from. Where her mother was from. I understood that. And I tried to be as accommodating as possible."

Finally, he did pause long enough to swallow a sip of water. "Mia had no school for a couple of days back in November. In service days or something, I can't remember exactly. But I decided it would be a good time to fly to Burgovnia. The plan was to spend a few days with my wife's family, and then fly back home. Simple, right?"

He picked up the wadded paper napkin again. One corner tore, but he didn't seem to notice; he just kept rolling it between his fingers.

"Anica was so upset that we weren't staying longer. I explained that Mia had started kindergarten. That we had to be back in the States by Monday. She was so annoyed that she wasn't able to enjoy the few days she did have with Mia. Anica is single. She never married. Has no children of her own. And I don't mind saying, her father has given her everything so it's difficult for her to take no for an answer. She made me feel like I was some kind of monster. That I was keeping her away from her only sister's only child, living over here in America while they were nearly half a world away."

Anguish carved itself into his expression, and Heather wanted to reach out to him. But she feared if she did, he might stop talking, and it was that intense need to hear his story that kept her hands on her side of the table.

"Anica got up on Saturday," he told her, "seeming to have made a complete turn-around. In attitude, I mean. She was cheerful. Friendly toward me. Her anger was gone, and I was grateful. It was like she finally realized she only had a short time left with Mia and that she should make the most of it."

He took a deep breath, but every muscle in his body seemed tight as a coiled spring.

"She announced she was taking Mia shopping for the day. My gut reaction was to insist on going along with them, but my father-in-law convinced me that having Mia to herself would help Anica. That it would give her some one-on-one memories to hold on to after we were gone." Daniel rested his forearms on the edge of the table, his fists clenching. "They didn't come back."

"Oh, Daniel." She could no more have kept herself from reaching out to him than she could have stopped time and tide.

The cotton cable knit of his sweater was soft under her fingers as she slid them over the back of his wrist. Nearly in one, efficient movement, he released the napkin, turned his hand over, and shifted it so that her fingers now glided neatly over his palm. His hand was warm and strong against hers, and they both held on tightly.

The anguish he must have been enduring, all these weeks of not knowing where his little girl has been. Heather couldn't imagine such torment.

"Are the police over there involved?" she asked. "Are they looking for Mia? Have they questioned your father-in-law? Can you get our government involved?" Finally, she blurted, "Why aren't you over there?"

Each question ramped up his distress to a higher level until his eyes glistened with wretchedness.

"Daniel, I'm so sorry." Emotion knotted in her throat. "I didn't mean to sound accusatory. It's just that... I can't imagine any parent..."

Heather let the rest of her comment die as it would only turn into another sharp dagger to wound him further. She pressed her lips together and blinked back the empathetic tears that burned her eyes.

"It's okay." His voice was a hoarse whisper. "Your questions are all very logical. Reasonable." He gave her hand a little supportive squeeze.

"Yes." He nodded. "The police over there are searching for Anica and Mia. They questioned everyone very early on, me, Jakob, the household staff, neighbors, relatives, friends. The police were trying to work in an unofficial capacity. You see, Jakob is a high-ranking government official and he didn't want his daughter's actions to be documented in any kind of official report." A frown bit deeply into his brow. "He begged me to keep things as quiet as possible. But when we woke up Sunday morning—the day Mia and I had planned to fly home—and Anica still hadn't returned, I nearly lost my mind. On Monday, the police confirmed that Anica had made a large cash withdrawal from her bank account. We know it was Anica, and not some kidnapper. The bank's surveillance camera caught her, clear as day. Mia was with her."

She couldn't take her eyes off his pained expression.

"It was clear to me," he went on, "that Anica wasn't intending to come back on her own. That we had to go out and find her. Find my daughter. Jakob disagreed with me and we argued. He was certain Anica would do the right thing if we just gave her time. While I believed that each moment we weren't searching was giving her that much more time to put distance between us."

Daniel swallowed and sighed. "I truly believe that Anica loves Mia. I do. And I'm certain that she wouldn't harm my daughter. I even understand that maybe I was wrong about going over there with the idea of only staying a few days. I should have given them more time together. The culture over there has some odd customs where family is concerned. Children don't normally live apart from their parents, even after they marry and have children of their own. So Anica felt Cila and I had broken tradition when we married and Cila moved to the States." Anger suddenly honed a sharp edge on his tone. "But that doesn't give Anica the right to take off with Mia without my permission."

"You're right," Heather agreed. "She has no right to do what she's doing. No right at all."

"I slipped away from the house Tuesday morning." He glanced out the front window. "I called around to some trusted friends. And I ended up hiring the same private detective agency that searched for Madeleine McCann when she went missing in Portugal. They haven't been able to find Maddie, but they'll find Mia. I'm sure of it. I have much more information about Mia's abductor than the McCanns had to work with."

He turned his head a fraction, his eyes latching onto Heather's as he repeated, "I'm sure they'll find Mia."

"Of course, they will."

He looked so utterly distraught. "Jakob was furious that I'd hired the detectives and we argued again. I threatened to go to the media if he didn't file a formal complaint with the police. And that's when I found myself escorted to the airport by three officials. Jakob rode with us and he never shut up during the twenty minutes it took to get there. Over and over again, he calmly assured me he'd find Mia. He told me I could keep my PIs on the case so long as they worked with the police. He told me my leaving the country was necessary. I was causing problems for the police, he said. My behavior—rogue behavior, is how he described it—was taking men away from the search."

Daniel raked his fingers through his hair. "All of that was a bunch of bullshit, of course. He just didn't want to have to press formal charges against his daughter, and that's exactly what I tried to persuade him to do."

Heather felt the pain, fear, and anger pulsing off him in waves. She gripped his hand in a feeble show of understanding. Of course, she didn't understand. Not completely. How could she? She'd never experienced anything as horrendous as this.

"They booted you out of the country," she breathed, the reiteration more for herself than him. The situation was astonishing. Something one would expect to read about in some crazy thriller novel, not a real life happening. "I can't believe it. It sounds absolutely crazy."

"I called my State Senator's office while I was still flying over the Atlantic," he told her. "I felt helpless, Heather. Utterly helpless. I didn't know what else to do. I was met at JFK by an official from the State Department. Dawson is his name. Tim Dawson. I couldn't believe they moved so fast."

"What has this Tim Dawson done? Did he contact the FBI? The CIA?" She had no idea how governments worked together on a crisis such as this. And if Jakob Brankov refused to lodge a formal complaint about the kidnapping—that's what this was, wasn't it, a kidnapping—then how could the two governments work together to find the child?

"All I can say is, Jakob must have friends in some very high places."

Daniel's voice sounded tired, and Heather's heart ached for him.

"What do you mean?" she asked. "Our government isn't helping you?"

"Oh, no. They're helping. They've sent a team of investigators. But everything is all under the radar. Tim keeps saying we need to avoid an international incident. He hinted that the US is in discussions with Burgovnia. I suspect it's over oil, but I can't be sure. But that's why the State Department wants to keep a lid on this mess. Tim keeps stressing that the Burgovnia police are working on it, my detectives are working on it, and the US Government is working on it. I talk to Tim at least twice a week. I talk to my detectives every day. And Jakob and I talk often, too, and every time I do, he says the same thing... that Anica loves Mia, and that we'll find them. That Mia will be home with me soon."

Heather had heard him talking in his room. She'd thought he was reading his day's writing aloud, or recording notes. She never imagined that all this time he was dealing with this unbelievably horrifying situation.

He seemed all talked out, bereft of both information and emotion. But Heather only felt more anxious.

"So Sandra Douglas, the girl I met with this morning, might be close to making your situation even worse than it already is." Heather inhaled deeply in an attempt to relax the tension that had built up in her shoulders.

"No one I know will talk to her," Daniel said. "I came here because an AP journalist came snooping around up in New York. I needed to get out of town. When my agent booked your place for the winter, I told him spending all that money was foolish. That this would be over in just a few days. That Mia would be back home in no time. But it was a good cover story, I figured. My staying here for the winter to finish my book." His gaze went flat as he added, "I never imagined Anica could be so good at dodging everyone who's looking for her. These have been the longest six weeks of my life."

"I'm sure they have been." She held his hand in both of hers, and as she stared into his face, she could tell he understood and appreciated the empathy she felt. If they had been in a more private place, she wouldn't have hesitated pulling him to her, doing her best to hug away his pain.

"Neither of you have eaten," Cathy said.

Heather started, unaware that Cathy had approached the table until she had spoken.

Cathy asked, "Is something wrong with the food?"

"Of course not." Sliding her hands away from Daniel, Heather smiled up at Cathy. "The soup is fine. It's good. Just like it always is."

"How would you know?" Cathy's brows arched slightly. "You haven't touched it. Your spoon looks like it just came out of the dishwasher."

"I tasted the soup, Cathy. We got busy talking is all." Heather slid out of the booth and tugged at the hem of her sweater. "Can I get some take-out containers? I'll box this up and we can eat it later."

Cathy cast her a narrow-eyed glance and then walked back behind the counter.

Heather told Daniel, "We should go. I love Cathy dearly, but she can be nosy sometimes. If we stay, she'll start poking into your business."

He got up and picked up his coat. "You don't think she'd talk to—"

"No way," Heather assured him. "Sandra

Douglas came sniffing around here before she came to see me and Cathy sent her packing."

Daniel nodded and stood out of the way while Cathy and Heather packed up their lunch. Then Heather grabbed her purse to pay, but Daniel pulled out his wallet and handed several bills to Cathy.

"Don't heat up those sandwiches in the microwave," Cathy warned. "They'll turn into a soggy mess."

Heather took the bag of food and shrugged the strap of her purse onto her shoulder. "What do think I am, an idiot? I'll crisp them up in a skillet, sweetie. Don't worry."

The keen interest blatantly written on Cathy's face had nothing to do with reheating grilled cheese sandwiches, Heather knew without a doubt. A tiny shadow of worry niggled at the back of her mind. The question wasn't *if* Cathy would ask about the conversation she and Daniel had had, the question was *when* Cathy would ask. Heather had never lied to Cathy or Sara about anything. Ever. However, for the first time in her life she found herself considering keeping Daniel's plight from her friends. It wasn't that she didn't trust them with the information. Her faith in them was implicit, and she'd proven that over the years as there wasn't a single thing about her they didn't know. But this was different.

It wasn't her secret to tell. This was Daniel's private life. This was his personal tragedy. She had no business sharing it with anyone.

He'd confided in her. He'd revealed himself—his pain and anguish. He'd opened up. Made himself vulnerable. And those facts left Heather feeling warm inside. As if they'd shared something deeply intimate.

Daniel walked out of the restaurant and Heather paused at the door, turning back and witnessing yet again the curiosity brightening Cathy's gaze. And when Cathy mouthed the words *call me*, Heather shot her a flat-lipped smile that offered no promises.

CHAPTER EIGHT

Heather had tossed and turned for more than an hour; it must be close to midnight. Weak winter moonlight shined through the window, painting the bedroom walls with a pale luster. The story about Daniel's daughter plagued her. She couldn't get the child out of her thoughts. Their talk had continued after they'd left the café. Daniel's best guess had been that his sister-in-law was doing everything she could to keep Mia occupied with fun and adventure, that Anica had to be obsessively keeping Mia entertained with new places and probably lots of gifts. He did his best to imagine that Mia was so busy that she wasn't even missing him. He hoped his little girl wasn't aware that the police and private detectives were actively searching for her. Heather prayed Daniel was right. She wished there was something she could say, something she could do, to help Daniel through this awful situation.

The idea that tormented Heather the most was when Daniel voiced his worry about what Anica might be saying to Mia about him. It was only natural that a child would worry about and fret over being separated from her father. How might Anica explain that separation, he'd wondered. She certainly couldn't tell Mia the truth. So what sort of lies was she conjuring?

Lines of strain had dug deep crevices in Daniel's face, and the memory disturbed Heather to the point that she threw back the quilt and sat up on the edge of the mattress. Suddenly, what was normally the soft, welcoming confines of her bed felt like solitary confinement in a cement block prison. She had to get up, had to move around, so that she could breathe. How on earth had he lived with this situation and remained sane all these weeks?

A little voice in the back of her head whispered, *what other choice did he have?*

Sooner or later, and she hoped to God it was sooner, little Mia would be found and returned home. Daniel had to remain strong, had to keep his mind and his body healthy, in order to take care of his daughter when that time arrived.

Heather slid her bare feet into her slippers and pushed her arms into her robe even as she moved toward the door. The wooden banister was cool to the touch as she made her way down the stairs. When she passed through the living room on her way to the kitchen, movement near the sofa made her steps slow. Daniel had swiveled his head to look at her, his features half illuminated by the pale light shafting through the front window.

"Can't sleep?" he asked.

She shook her head.

"Me, either."

"I was going to make myself some herbal tea," she told him. "Want a cup?"

He smiled and nodded. "That would be nice. Thanks."

"I must have half a dozen different flavors. Lemon, mint, strawberry, goji berry..."

His smile widened just a fraction. "Surprise me."

"I can do that."

Having a mission made her feel less helpless, and it wasn't long before she was carrying two steaming mugs into the living room and settling herself next to him.

"Do you want me to turn on a light?" she asked.

"I'd rather you didn't." He set his mug on the coffee table without taking a sip. "I actually get a little comfort from sitting in the moonlight."

Emotion welled in her chest, forceful and profound, pinching her heart and burning her eyes. She leaned forward and carefully placed her mug on the table next to his, the overwhelming compassion surging through her making her trembly. She turned to him, moistening her lips and swallowing.

"Daniel..." Her mouth pressed into a firm line as she tried to find the words to express her feelings. Finally, she shook her head. "I can't even find the words to describe how terrible I feel about what you're going through."

"Oh, sweetheart." He whispered the words.

Shifting on the sofa, he took both her hands in his. "Listen to me. I'm sorry that you feel badly. It wasn't my intention to cause you—"

"Please don't apologize to me, Daniel," she blurted. Her sight became watery. "And don't worry about me either. Not for a single second. You have enough trouble to deal with."

The corners of his mouth curled softly and his shoulders rounded. He reached up and brushed away the tear that rolled down her cheek.

"You've become my angel, Heather. My saving grace. I was just sitting here thinking about you."

Her first impulse was to negate what he was saying, but he didn't give her a chance.

"I had *no idea* how badly I needed to talk about all of this," he continued. "It feels so *good* to finally be able to tell someone about all this... crap. About all this darkness and anxiety and... and utter frustration."

"I don't know how you've done it," she said. "I don't know how you've held yourself together all this time."

"There were days I felt as if I was holding on by my fingernails, gritting my teeth, as I waited for some kind of news, some little bit of information on how the search was going." He squeezed her fingers. "But now, even though I'm still in the midst of this disaster, I don't feel so... alone."

"You're not," she insisted. "You're not alone. I mean that."

They stared at each other, and with each silent second that passed, the moment grew more meaningful, more intimate.

"I have never in my life met anyone like you, Heather." He pulled her hands closer to him, resting them on his thigh. "You are kind. I'm not talking about sympathetic. Anyone can show concern for a short while. But you're..." He paused a moment. "You're gracious. And you're generous with that graciousness. I mean, hell, you open your home to complete strangers."

His compliments discomfited her. "Wait, now. Those strangers pay me to stay—"

"I'm not talking about your guests," he said, cutting her off. "I'm not talking about business courtesies. I mean true benevolence. Like the warm-hearted manner in which you opened your home to that little girl and her family on Christmas Eve. You didn't hesitate. You invited Izzie in. You invited all of them in, and you made sure they felt welcome. At ease. At home."

His gaze lowered as he murmured, "Izzie made me realize that, even though I might not know where my daughter is, I am still truly blessed that Mia is physically healthy. She's not fighting some horrible illness."

The memory of Izzie's peach-colored bald head made Heather remember the depth of tender emotions she'd felt for the child and her parents that night, and she'd thought about them many times since then, too.

"You are so wonderfully unassuming," Daniel said, lifting his chin to look into her eyes. "You always seem to put everyone else's needs before your own. Those of your guests. Your friends. Even those of strangers. That kind of selflessness is damned unique."

She wanted to speak, wanted to refute all the things he was saying, but the lump that had swelled in her throat prevented her from saying a single word. The fact that he thought such wonderful things about her brought her great joy. And even greater fear. Heather didn't have time to contemplate why that might be before he spoke again.

"And you're absolutely beautiful."

Her fear turned to terror and she shook her head.

"You *are*," he stressed. "Your eyes are lovely. Your skin glows. Your silky hair makes me want to comb my fingers through all those soft curls."

It was as if, in saying the words, he'd given himself permission to touch her. And he did—hesitantly, gently. He slid his hand along the side of her head, stroking her hair and her cheek, his dark eyes never leaving hers.

He leaned toward her and whispered, "You're beautiful, Heather. You are. Inside and out."

Desire propelled her forward, but the momentum came with excruciating slowness. A fraction of an inch at a time, it seemed, until finally, their mouths met.

Heather surrendered to the luscious need coursing through her. His moist, hot lips tasted delicious, and she felt her body relax against him.

She had lived in a state of resistance until her self-denial of all things sexual had become innate, completely natural and inherent. Being with

Daniel, feeling his fingertips on her face, tasting his kisses, had slowly made her aware of the magnitude of restraint she'd practiced for so long when it came to sensual matters.

He deepened the kiss, tasting her lips, her tongue, putting just enough pressure so as to have her leaning against the sofa's back. His hands were on her body, sliding down the curve of her neck, the length of her arm, and coming to rest on her belly.

"Come upstairs with me," he pleaded.

Pure, carnal need pulsed at the apex of her thighs. She wanted this man. Desperately. She wanted to touch him, to feel his skin beneath her fingertips, to trace the paths of his corded muscles with the flat of her palm. She wanted to spend hours making love with him, wanted to lose herself in a long night of sweaty sheets and satiated need.

Daniel planted small, succulent kisses along her jaw, buried his face in her hair as he nuzzled and tasted her neck. She closed her eyes and released a soft groan.

She wanted this. Oh, how she *wanted* this.

He slid his hand up her abdomen and over to her side until he cupped her breast in his palm.

The heat of him penetrated her robe and her nightgown, stirring her anxiety.

Still inebriated with gnawing hunger for him, she tried to ignore the apprehension that budded inside her.

Maybe she could slip into the bathroom and put on some sexy lingerie. Maybe then, if she didn't remove her bra, he wouldn't notice. Maybe if she were to—

But the cold, hard truth persisted, seeping in, bone deep, chilling her longing. The attraction they felt might distract him for a while. Their love-making might divert his attention. She might even make it through the rosy afterglow of lying in his arms, sated and spent. But eventually he would notice. At some point he would see.

And he would be horrified.

At last, reality snuffed out every vestige of her passion.

She tensed in his embrace, and he noticed immediately. He leaned away from her and she took the opportunity to act. In one swift motion, she grasped his wrist and removed his hand from her body, and then pulled her robe up over her shoulder where it had fallen loose.

"I can't do this, Daniel." Her jaw had gone so tense it hurt, but it wasn't nearly as painful as the anguish that clutched her heart in a death-grip.

Confusion shadowed his black eyes. "I'm sorry. Did I—"

"You didn't do anything. You didn't. I promise you. It's just that... I can't..." Her exhalation was shaky. "I just can't do this."

The sound of plastic vibrating against wood drew their gazes to where his cell phone sat on the coffee table.

"I'll let you get that." She started to get up, but his hand clamped down on her forearm.

"I have to take this. You know I do. But please don't go anywhere. Please."

The pleading in his eyes was her ruin. Her breath left her in a rush, and she yielded to him with a small nod.

He snatched up the phone and went to stand by the picture window. Heather heard him offer a curt greeting, and then he turned his back to her, his tone dropping to a murmur.

The call was a relief, really, as it gave her a moment to collect her thoughts.

Her first inclination had been to escape, to flee

him and the irresistible yearning his kiss, his touch stirred in her. Oh, how she wanted him. However, when she began to imagine being with him, the idea morphed into a razor sharp focus of his blanched expression, the repulsion she would witness in his eyes, when he looked on her nakedness.

Rather than feeling panicked, she went dead calm inside. Now that she had been given time to pause and reflect, she realized she cared about this man. Cared about what he thought of her. Deeply. She wanted him to understand why she wasn't willing to engage in a physical relationship with him.

Less than half a minute later, he ended the call and turned back to her.

Light from the window set his dark hair glowing and cast his face in shadow, so it was impossible for her to read his expression.

"Did you learn anything?" she asked. "Good news?"

He moved to the sofa and sat down. "They seem certain that they're on the right trail. They've just missed her, they think. They've been just missing her for what feels like a lifetime." He shook his head. "In the beginning days, everyone was certain that one of Anica's friends was allowing her to hide out. But my detectives questioned dozens of people. The police did, too."

Heather laced her fingers and tucked her clasped hands into her lap. "How on earth is your father-in-law keeping this out of the newspapers over there, Daniel? I mean, the police are talking to people, your detectives are talking to people, the State Depart—"

"Burgovnia isn't a democracy, Heather." His statement was spoken in a low murmur. "The citizens there don't enjoy the same kinds of freedoms that we have here."

She let out a soft sigh of frustration, the idea of human rights and freedoms conjuring memories from the social science class she'd taken when she'd attended the local community college. She'd never forget the look of pride on her teacher's face when the woman had told the room full of students about Franklin D. Roosevelt's 1941 State of the Union address. The Four Freedoms Speech, as the address came to be known, proposed that people everywhere in the world should have freedom of speech, freedom of worship, freedom from want, and freedom from fear. That teacher had instilled in Heather a deep appreciation for both the US Constitution and the Bill of Rights.

"The government keeps a tight rein on what the press can and can't print," he said.

"It's just so unfair. If the newspapers there would run Anica's picture or Mia's picture, surely someone would see them. And what about social media? You could post photos. Ask for information. Surely, you have fans in Eastern Europe. Someone would contact you with information about your sister-in-law's location."

"I've already explained," he said. "I was warned by my contact at the State Department. Dawson said not to stir things up. Not to make trouble for Jakob. I've been assured that they're doing all they can to find my daughter."

Daniel took her hands in his, and only when she felt the warmth of his fingers still in hers did she realize that at some point, she'd begun digging the pad of her left thumb into the palm of her right hand. The spot burned from the friction.

"They are going to find them," he told her. "They're going to find them soon. My guy said that

Anica and Mia had left the hotel today so quickly, that one of Mia's sweaters was left behind."

Since Anica had fled so suddenly, Heather thought, the woman must be frazzled. Maybe she would make a mistake soon. Maybe she would say something telling to a stranger—a gas station attendant, a hotel clerk, someone—that would lead the detectives to her.

Daniel repeated, "They're going to find them."

Heather nodded.

Still holding onto her hands, he scooted closer to her. "Now that my phone call is over, I need you to tell me what's going on." He searched her face. "Tell me why you won't let me make love to you."

CHAPTER NINE

She had thought she was ready. Of course, she hadn't had time to process the exact words she would use, but just moments ago she'd been certain that she wanted him to understand her thoughts and feelings, she wanted him to know about her... situation.

Now, looking into his anxious face, the idea of providing an explanation seemed to disappear from her mind in a vaporous *pcof*, like the coin that vanished with the snap of a magician's fingers.

He reached up and brushed her hair back from her shoulder. "Talk to me, Heather. I want you. I know you know that. And I can tell you want me too." He paused, his head tilting just a bit. "This isn't the first time you've frozen up on me. You enjoy our kisses just as much as I do." He smiled. "I know you do. I can hear it in your breathing, feel it in your quickening pulse. So please talk to me. Help me to understand what's going on. Tell me what you're afraid of."

What *was* she afraid of? It was a simple enough answer. She was afraid for him to look at her body. Afraid of the revulsion she'd see in his eyes.

"The truth is, Daniel," she began, "I don't like my body."

"How can that be? You're curvy. Lush. Beautiful. Sexy as hell." He smiled. "Do you need more adjectives?"

She lowered her gaze.

"You *have* had sex before..." Then he hurriedly added, "I mean, of course you've—"

Now she smiled. She couldn't help it. "I'm no virgin. I was once engaged to be married."

He nodded but remained silent.

"Steve left me, though. And it was all my fault.

It was my choice to make and, well, I made it." She offered a tiny shrug.

Clearly, Daniel had no clue what she was trying to explain.

She sighed, the idea of dredging up all those bad memories made her feel exhausted. But she steeled herself. He deserved to know the truth.

"Ten years ago, my mother was diagnosed with breast cancer. It was a very difficult time for her." Her gaze wandered to the far side of the room, searching the shadows. "Steve was so good through the whole thing. He drove Mom to a lot of her appointments. When she became really sick, he helped me get her in and out of the house. I swear, cancer treatment is absolute torture. I watched Mom shrink into all that suffering right before my very eyes."

Grim and frightening images whorled through Heather's mind. Her mother's pale complexion, her hollow eyes, her ever-decreasing physical strength.

"At first," she continued, "it looked as though the treatments were working." She pressed her lips together for a moment. "All of us thought everything would be okay. I know that Steve loved me, of course, but I do believe he asked me to marry him more as a means of lifting my mom's spirits, getting her to fight her way back to health." She looked at Daniel, a faint smile curving her lips. "It was a nice thing he did. Mom did rally for a bit after that. But she relapsed really quickly."

Daniel's expression remained impassive. Why would it be anything else? She was so far from the point in her story that would answer his question.

"Mom only survived three and half years after being diagnosed."

He stared at her for a long moment. "I'm very sorry for your loss. Grieving for those we've loved and lost is... a very difficult process. But, Heather, honey—" He gave a small shake of his head. "—I honestly don't understand how this..."

"Please be patient with me. This is hard. I'm getting there. I promise." In need of a little security, she crossed her arms, cupping her elbows in her palms and drawing them inward. "Before my mom died, she begged me to be tested." Heather moistened her lips. "Have you heard of the BRCA1 and BRCA2 gene mutations?"

Surprisingly, he nodded. "I did some research.

For one of the characters in a book I wrote some time ago. You tested positive?"

"BRCA1. The doctor said I had a 65% chance of being diagnosed with breast cancer." Her heart rate shot skyward, and her mouth went dry. But she was determined to finish this. "I opted to have a double mastectomy."

He eased himself against the sofa back. "You obviously had reconstructive surgery, yes?" Before she could answer, he said, "Forgive me for being so blunt, but that was warm, live flesh I cupped in my hand before..."

Raging heat scorched her face and neck, and she found it impossible to look at him.

"Reconstructive surgery. Yes." She grimaced. "I guess you could call it that."

"Heather, you said your fiancé left you because you made a choice." He leaned forward, bracing his elbows on his knees. "Are you saying that jackass broke off your engagement because you chose to save your life?"

She hefted one shoulder in a tiny shrug. "From his perspective, the 35% chance of remaining cancer free looked pretty good. And I would have been whole. Undamaged."

"What the hell? You *are* whole."

There was anger in his gaze; she could feel it burning into her even though she kept her eyes averted.

"So... are you saying you haven't had a relationship since? Are you letting him and his stupid ideas about what you should or shouldn't have done with your own body—*your own body*—keep you from having a loving relationship with anyone else?"

Before she could say another word, his spine went straight as a steel rod.

"Are you lumping me in with that jackass? Do you think that I would—"

The tone of his voice scared her, conjured all manner of twisted memories of arguing about her decision to have surgery all those years ago.

She stood up. "Daniel, stop! I didn't intend to make you angry. I only meant to explain why I can't... why we can never..."

Hot tears splintered her vision, and she was grateful that they had chosen to leave the lamps turned off. Hopefully, the shadowy darkness would keep him from seeing just how upset she was.

"I just wanted you to know that... *I can't do this.*"

Then she turned away from him and hurried from the room.

~*~

The Sunshine Grill was one of those quaint little eateries that locals clung to and tourists fell in love with deeply enough to return to during all seasons of the year. It was the kind of place you wanted to visit, not just to chow down on a stack of hot blueberry pancakes dripping with butter and served with a side of crispy bacon, but because you knew you would more than likely see your friends there. You could watch the daily news or read the Dispatch, and there was always someone around interested in discussing what was happening in the world. Daniel knew he would use The Grill, or a place very much like it, in a future book.

He sat in a booth, the cup of coffee on the table in front of him having grown as cold as the winter wind that whipped across the beach outside. Cathy had refilled the cup twice, and he'd declined a third. The caffeine he'd consumed already had his insides jittery.

He continued to bide his time, patiently waiting

for the mid-morning lull. Only one customer, other than himself, remained in the café, and the elderly gentleman was just now pulling out his wallet and handing money to Cathy to pay his bill. The old guy offered his boisterous goodbyes, told Cathy he'd see her tomorrow, and even gave Daniel a quick nod before zipping his coat and walking out into the sunny but chilly January day.

His idea to talk to Heather's friends probably wasn't a good one. But he'd messed up badly last night when Heather had left him stewing in his own anger. He shouldn't have snapped at her; he shouldn't have let his emotions take control. Of his thoughts. And of his tone. He'd grown incensed on Heather's behalf when he'd learned how her fiancé had treated her. And then he'd completely lost it the instant he'd realized that Heather had obviously concluded that he—Daniel—would treat her just as callously as that jackass Steve had done. Like a Lamborghini Murcielago with a lead-footed driver, his temper had shot into high gear before he could grapple it under control. She had cut their conversation off with the stern censure that had narrowed her gaze and tightened the muscles around her mouth. And she'd walked away from him.

Yes, he'd screwed up royally. She'd barely spoken to him at breakfast. He'd tried to apologize, but she'd shut him down.

So now, he was looking for some way to fix things. And he'd decided that, in order to do that, he needed more information.

Daniel slid out of the booth, grabbed his cup, and made his way to the counter that ran three-quarters of the way across the back of the restaurant. Cathy was busy emptying clean dishes from the plastic rack that sat next to the industrial dishwasher. When she noticed him, she called, "You change your mind about more coffee?"

Automatically, she stopped what she was doing.

"No. Actually, Cathy... I'd like to talk to you. If you don't mind." He set the thick ceramic cup onto the counter. "I've been... waiting. For your morning customers to clear out."

"I'm a little busy," she hedged.

He could clearly see she was uncertain about his request.

"I have things to do to get ready for the lunch crowd."

"We can talk while you work, if you want." He slid onto a stool and rested his hands on the counter top in a gentle attempt to let her know he wasn't going anywhere, and he hoped like hell she didn't flat out refuse him.

She reached down and grabbed the bottom corner of her white apron and dried her hands on the fabric, a purely habitual action as her hands weren't even wet. Leaving the remaining dishes in the rack, she made her way toward him.

"Who am I kidding?" She gave a little humorous huff. "The lunch crowd will consist of a dozen or so grizzled old dudes who'll insist on harassing me about the freshness of the tuna salad. But the joke's going to be on them today. There *is* no tuna salad. I made chicken salad this morning. They'll have to eat it and like it, or go someplace else for lunch."

Cathy stopped in front of him on the far side of the counter.

"So what's this about?" she asked.

The light in her eyes held both curiosity and hesitation. Her uncertainty was palpable.

The counter top was a stark white beneath his

widely splayed fingers. He hadn't realized he was so tense.

"Look," he began, "I realize you don't like me much. I don't understand why. I'm sure I must have done something along the line to earn your disapproval, but I'd like to apologize for, you know, whatever it was."

She frowned, her chin tucking back sharply. "You're apologizing to me, but you don't know what you're apologizing for? That's a little odd, don't you think?"

Her questions took him aback, and for a moment, he hadn't a single iota how to respond.

"Me?" She placed her hand on her chest. "I think it's a rather strange thing for you to do. Why do you care if I like you or not?"

"To tell you the truth—" he paused long enough to ponder whether or not to finish his sentence, then he decided to let it roll. "I don't."

She smiled. "There you go. That's what I thought. Now we're getting somewhere."

Daniel sat up straight and pulled his hand back until his wrists were resting on the corner of the counter, his mouth pulling downward.

"Why are you so... disagreeable?"

Her grin widened. "Forgive me, but I think the two of us were pretty much agreeable just now."

His shoulders rounded with a sigh.

"I mean, look," she told him, planting a hand on her hip, "you came in here and said you're sorry for doing something to make me dislike you, but you don't even know what it is that might have—"

"Stop!" He felt the fingers on both his hands go straight again. The woman was making this hellishly frustrating. "The apology was a gesture, okay? A token. An offering."

"I don't get it. Why would you need to offer me anything?"

He felt his jaw tense. "Think of it this way. We're two countries, see? Two countries that don't get along all that well. One wants something from the other, right? So they don't go in and just make a cold request. That would be undiplomatic. They make a gesture. Offer some sort of token first. Ease the path to good relations."

"Thank you for the civics lesson. I didn't realize we were still in high school." She shifted her weight. "So your token to ease the path to a better relationship between us is to say you're sorry for... For? *You don't even know what.*" She groused, "What you should apologize for is getting on my last nerve."

"Okay, I admit it. My gesture was a little empty."

"So now that we've agreed a second time," she said, "what is it you want to talk about? Just spit it out, already."

He inhaled slowly. "It's about Heather. I'm worried about her."

Cathy remained silent.

"She and I have gotten close these past few weeks. Because you and she are such good friends, she's probably already told you how close." Cathy's steady gaze made him uncomfortable, so he gazed off into the kitchen. "Really..." He forced himself to look into Cathy's eyes as he finished, "Close."

"Come on." Her brows arched. "Not that close. I know Heather pretty well."

"True. But not because we haven't... wanted to." He swallowed. "Be. That close. I mean."

"We're both adults here, Daniel. We can say the word sex and not be cast into the bowels of hell." Her expression turned pointed.

"You're right."

When he didn't offer more, she said, "So...

you're saying that you and Heather have wanted to have sex. But you haven't had sex."

"Exactly. And I need to know why."

Cathy crossed her arms. "Don't you think that's something you should ask Heather?"

He nodded. "We did talk. She did tell me. A lot, actually. But she didn't tell me enough. Because I still don't understand."

The delicate skin around Cathy's eyes tightened as she contemplated what he said.

"Heather told me about her jackass of a fiancé."

"Steve," she murmured.

"Yes. And that he left her." Daniel tugged lightly on his pinky finger. "She told me about her mother's breast cancer diagnosis. She told me about helping her mom through the cancer treatment, and how her mother died three years after being diagnosed."

The commiseration emanating from Cathy told him that the friends had gone through the whole ordeal together.

"And Heather told me about testing positive for BRCA1."

Cathy's gaze widened slightly, but she didn't say a word.

"She told me about the operation. The double mastectomy."

Her lips parting, Cathy gasped. "She told you about the scars?"

Agitation had him ticking off all he knew as if the facts were items on a grocery list. But her question silenced him.

"What are you talking about? What scars?"

The color drained from her face, and ever so slowly, she brought her lips together, then pressed them tight between her teeth.

"Cathy?" he urged. "What are you talking about? I know Heather had reconstructive surgery..." He shook his head slowly. "But she didn't mention anything about scars."

Her eyelids rolled closed. "Oh, my. What the hell have I done?" she groaned out the words softly, almost to herself. She pressed the fingers of both her hands to her bloodless mouth and looked up toward the ceiling. Her gaze went shiny and were suddenly rimmed with a deep pink.

"Daniel, you can't tell her I told you. She will never forgive me, do you hear me? Never."

Her agony scattered with the force of buckshot, trumping his need for more information about what she'd said. If he didn't calm Cathy's distress, he was sure she would shut down and refuse to tell him anything more.

"Look," he said, keeping his tone calm even though his insides were in a flurry, "I'm not going to say a word to Heather. I promise you. I'm not going to tell Heather anything. You can trust me on that."

Tears glistened in Cathy's eyes now, and he watched her hands tremble.

"You can't say a word."

Her gaze darted from his face, to the front door, to the cash register, yet Daniel knew she wasn't really seeing anything; she was so swallowed up by her guilt and anguish.

"She won't let anyone see," Cathy whispered. "Even after the operation. Sara and I helped get her through that awful time. She was so sore...so... wounded. Physically and emotionally. She refused to let us check her bandages. A-and, and...even after she healed, she became so self-conscious... so protective of her body. Once, we were out shopping. I found a dress I thought she'd love. I didn't even think about it; I walked into her dressing room. She was wearing a bra, for goodness sake. I didn't see anything more than a flash of bare shoulders and chest. But she was mortified. I've never seen her so angry. She didn't speak to me for three weeks."

"It's going to be okay," he assured her. "I promise you."

"If she ever finds out, it won't be okay. I'm telling you. My friendship with Heather is on the line here."

Cathy had worked herself up to the point that Daniel worried about her. She was ghostly pale and shaking. He slid off the stool, and as he rounded the counter toward her, he said, "You've got to calm down. This isn't good for you."

He clasped her elbow and placed one hand on the small of her back, gently guiding her out into the dining room.

"You need to sit down. Relax. Let me make you a cup of tea."

She let him lead her, and she sat at the table nearest the counter.

"I'll put lots of sugar in it," he told her. "You'll feel better in no time. You'll see."

Just minutes later, the color had returned to Cathy's cheeks and she did look and seem less tense. Surprisingly, she'd continued to talk, continued to answer his questions. Her responses were brief, but he continued to pull small bits of information from her.

"A bilateral mastectomy," Cathy told him. "Search images on Google."

He nodded. "I have." And he explained about having done research on the subject for a book he'd written. "But, I'm guessing, her results don't match the pretty images I've seen."

"I'm guessing you'd be right." She sipped her tea, and then swallowed.

"I still don't understand. She told me she had reconstructive surgery."

"Sara and I found her sobbing one day. Years ago. She called herself disgusting. She revealed to us that her scars slashed across the center—" Cathy closed her eyes and shook her head. "She said her breasts looked—" Cathy heaved a heavy sigh "—as smooth as two water balloons."

Realization suddenly dawned on Daniel. Now he understood everything clearly. The surgeon had removed Heather's nipples.

"The truth is," Cathy said, emotional exhaustion softening her voice, "my beautiful friend doesn't feel beautiful. In fact, the opposite is true. She feels quite ugly."

His nod was meant to convey his full comprehension. He didn't say anything more. There was no more need for questions and probing. He knew all he needed to, and his heart was filled with such sadness for Heather.

"You're not going to tell her?"

The beseeching quality in Cathy's eyes, in her tremulous question, touched him to the very marrow.

How could he let Heather know that none of this mattered to him if he didn't tell her he knew? What she saw as a physical abnormality would never bother him one whit. But how would she ever come to understand that if he remained silent?

He reached across the table and encircled her wrist with his fingers. "Listen to me, Cathy. I swear to you that I will never tell Heather that you and I talked. I won't. You can trust me. I mean it."

She visibly relaxed, and she even gave him a small smile of thanks.

After a moment, she asked, "So, why me? Why did you come to talk to me? Especially when you thought, you know, that we're two countries that don't get along and all that."

He had to grin.

"Why didn't you talk to Sara?" Cathy went on. "Most days, she's right next door. You've got to have noticed that she's far nicer than I am."

Daniel pulled his hand back to his side of the table. "Yeah, well, I wasn't looking for nice. I was looking for honest."

She seemed content with his answer.

CHAPTER TEN

Fake it till you make it. It wasn't an attitude that normally resonated with Heather. She preferred expressing honest emotions. But living in a place of truth just wasn't possible for her right now.

She wanted Daniel. Craved him. That was the truth.

Every night she dreamed about his hands skimming over her body, touching her in every dark, secret place, his eager kisses nearly bringing her to orgasm. She would wake up, gasping and sweaty and aching with need.

But that need would never be satiated. She would never tremble under his fingertips. She would never trail her fingers over the firm muscles of his naked body.

Never.

Her body might be weak, and her imagination—at least while she slept—might fail her, but her mind was made up.

When she'd told Daniel that she couldn't engage in a physical relationship with him, she'd meant it with every fiber of her being. The only thing waiting for her were she to relax her stance would be more humiliation than she would ever be able to bear.

So for the past few days, she'd faked it. She'd plastered on a smile and a happy disposition, and she'd played the efficient, cheerful host of The Lonely Loon. It wasn't difficult, and there were times when it didn't feel all that phoney—as long as she avoided that intense gaze of his. And little by little the ploy continued to work its magic. Her pleasant yet detached demeanor helped her maintain some space between herself and Daniel.

She didn't see him all that often, she now realized. The toughest part was the time she spent serving him breakfast.

She stood at the island in the kitchen, a juice pitcher and a carafe of coffee ready and waiting. Rather than choosing one, which would turn into two trips, she picked up both and headed toward the dining room. When she passed through the door, she contracted her cheek muscles and forced a smile onto her mouth.

Damn, he looked good. His black hair was still damp from his shower, and his clean-shaven face seemed to invite her to reach out and trace her fingers along his jaw. Thank goodness both her hands were full.

"I've got orange juice," she told him brightly. "And coffee. I'll fill you up with both, and then I'll leave you alone so you can eat in peace."

His gaze met hers, and she immediately focused on his juice glass. The air temperature rose, and she scrambled for something more to say.

"I can't believe it's nearly February."

He jerked or flinched; she wasn't sure which. Then the butter knife he'd reached for thumped on the table top.

Instinctively, she stopped pouring.

"What's the date?" he asked her, scrambling for his phone. "Aw, damn it."

Butter from the knife he'd dropped had smeared on his thumb and palm, and a glop of it now adorned the case of his cell phone.

Heather set down the coffee carafe, pulled free the tea towel that had been tucked into the waistband of her apron, and held it out to him. He ignored her.

"The date!" he repeated.

"It's the twenty-fifth."

Misery made his face go stark. He took the towel she offered, but he didn't use it to wipe off his hand or phone. He simply sat there, staring up at her.

"What is it, Daniel? What's wrong."

"It's her birthday." His lips were dry. "I can't believe I forgot. How could I have forgotten?"

"Mia's birthday?" The imaginary bricks she'd used to build her wall of protection seemed to crumble to dust the very instant she saw guilt snuff the light out of his eyes.

She set down the juice pitcher, pulled out a chair and sat down close to him. "Daniel, it's going to be all right."

"But you don't understand." Absently, he set the phone down and began swiping the greasiness from his hand. "Her birthday is *our* day. Together, I mean. Ever since her mom died, I've gone out of my way to make Mia's birthday special. I take off work. I plan an outing of some sort. We make a whole day it. Just Mia and me." He went quiet, shaking his head as he tossed the towel aside. "She's going to be so upset."

Heather could no more not reach out to him than she could keep herself from drawing breath. She slid her fingers over his forearm. "You'll make it up to her just as soon as she comes home. It won't be long. You've said that, over and over. And I believe you're absolutely right. It won't be long, Daniel. It won't be long."

Although the corners of his eyes still crinkled with distress, he offered her a tiny semblance of a smile, and Heather felt her insides grow molten, as if she were filled with hot, radiant sunlight.

And in that moment, she knew. This man was on the verge of stealing her heart. She could so easily fall in love with him. All the signs were there. She wanted him to be happy, wanted only good things, joyful things, for him. She wished to level out all the rough patches from his path. She wanted to make his way easy. Wanted to soothe his hurt, take away his pain.

Oh, Lord, she silently prayed, she was going to have to tread very carefully. Allowing herself to fall in love in the past had brought nothing but disastrous results—heartache and misery.

Blinking her way out of dreary thoughts that had sucked her in, she inhaled deeply and focused on his face, concentrated on easing his worry.

Her bolstering words seemed so weak and ineffectual. But that's all she could offer him. She couldn't bring his little girl home to him; and right now, that's the only thing that he longed for.

Daniel covered her hand with his, nodding his head. "You're right, of course," he told her. "It won't be long. And that means I have to be ready, right? I think I'll go out shopping. See if I can find a present or two."

Seemed like he, too, had decided on employing the fake-it-till-you-make-it attitude, and surprisingly, that made Heather smile.

"What a wonderful idea." Buying gifts for Mia would be the perfect plan to help him feel more in control of a miserably out-of-control situation.

"You could go to the outlets in West Ocean City. Or you could go to the Salisbury Mall. Or the Rehoboth Outlets. There are plenty of places to shop around here, that's for sure."

They talked for a few minutes longer, and he cleaned the mess off his phone while she gave him directions to Salisbury.

Soon, he was on his way upstairs to grab his car keys and coat, and she was left sitting at the dining room table. And that's when the idea came to her. While he was out looking for a surprise for his daughter, Heather would be busy making a surprise for him.

~*~

Three hours later, Heather hummed a cheery tune as she put the finishing touches on the birthday surprise. The two-layer vanilla cake she'd baked might be slightly on the boring side, but the outside was a work of art. She'd tinted the shiny marshmallow icing pink and used a liberal amount of rainbow-colored sprinkles on top. The resulting fluffy confection would have made any child feel special. Heather hoped Daniel thought so, anyway.

Party streamers and banners were standard supplies she kept on hand just in case her guests were celebrating a birthday or an anniversary during their stay and wanted an impromptu party. A colorful HAPPY BIRTHDAY banner swooped in an arc on the dining room wall, and crepe paper draped gracefully from the corners of the ceiling to the center-most point on the chandelier hanging over the table. The decorations weren't the fanciest, but they were enough to let Daniel know she supported him in his effort to celebrate Mia's birthday.

When Heather heard his key turn in the back door lock, she set the cake on the table and headed toward the kitchen to meet him. Automatically, her hands went to her hair and she combed her fingers through the long, soft curls. When she realized she was primping, she snatched the tea towel from the back of the kitchen chair to give herself something to hold on to. How she looked didn't matter. The important thing was what she had done.

"Hey," he said, smiling.

He carried several bags, one made of stiff brown

paper with braided jute handles, the others, plain white plastic.

Her gaze dipped to the front of her shirt and she checked for any errant dustings of flour or smudges of pink icing.

"Looks like you were successful." She heard the happy excitement in her own voice.

Daniel nodded as he made his way over to the table. "I found some things I think Mia will love." He set the bags on the table, inhaling deeply and gazing around at the mess she'd left in the kitchen.

"Smells good in here," he told her, taking in the batter-smeared and icing-encrusted bowls, unwashed baking pans, measuring cups, spoons, and spatulas that littered the counter tops along with the ingredients. "I've never seen the kitchen so... lived in."

Heather chuckled at his polite choice of words. He was right; cleaning up as she cooked was her normal practice. But while the cake had been baking in the oven, she'd been too busy decorating the dining room to wash up the bowls and utensils she'd used, or wipe up the drips of batter from the kitchen counter. And then she'd focused on icing the cake and making it pretty. No matter. She'd set the kitchen right soon enough.

"What's going on?"

A thrill shot through her as she anticipated his reaction to what she was about to unveil.

"I've got a surprise for you." She gave a slight jerk of her head toward the dining room. "Come on in here." Then she paused. "Bring Mia's gifts."

She hurried through the doorway and into the dining room, then she'd pivoted a hundred eighty degrees and took the last few steps backward so she could watch his face.

"Ta-da!" She spread her arms, palms facing upward.

The wonder on his handsome face was almost too much for her to bear. Her heart squeezed with a painful pleasure even though she could tell he was still uncertain about exactly what he was seeing.

"Wha...?" He gazed at the decorations and the cake. "Heather?" He looked into her eyes.

"It's a birthday party," she announced brightly. "For Mia."

"I can... see that. But I don't understand."

His words came haltingly and she laughed.

"You're going to set out Mia's gifts," she

explained. "We're going to light the candles and sing happy birthday." She reached over and picked up her cell from where she'd placed it on the buffet. "And I'm going to video the whole thing. With my phone. I'll text it to you so..." Her tone went quiet. "When you see your daughter, you can let her know you remembered. She'll see that you kept her and her day special. Even though the two of you couldn't be together. You celebrated... just like you always do."

For several long seconds he said nothing, only looked at her, and Heather felt a tiny spark of fear. Maybe she'd overstepped the bounds. Maybe she'd been presumptuous.

Maybe the party wasn't as good an idea as she'd imagined. Maybe a party would only make him miss Mia more.

Nerves danced in her belly. She tucked her top lip between her teeth, applying enough nervous pressure to cause her pain.

Maybe he felt celebrating without Mia would be utterly ridiculous.

And maybe he'd be right.

"Heather."

His voice was barely a whisper, but the sound

of it snapped her out of her miserable reverie and caused her to flinch. Thankfully, he didn't seem to notice.

He set the bags of gifts on the table and turned his full attention on her, lightly cupping his hands on her shoulders.

"This is the most wonderful idea I have ever heard."

His words along with the gratitude softening his features, snuffed out any semblance of fear she'd felt. He smiled down into her face.

The warmth of his skin permeated her blouse, and she became acutely aware of the scent of his cologne. Powerful vibrations pulsed from him. Veneration? Esteem? Adoration? Heather wasn't completely certain, but the discomfort she felt was a call to action and had her shrugging out of his embrace.

"Well, let's get this party started," she exclaimed, and then she immediately checked the volume of her tone.

She began pilfering in the bags he'd brought home.

"Aw, a teddy bear." She pulled the brown, fluffy

stuffed animal free, stroking his soft fur. "I love his coat. And look at that scarf."

"He has a suit," Daniel said. "And a pair of pajamas. Mia loves teddy bears."

"Daniel, it's perfect." She set the bear down and reached for the plastic bags. "And what's in these?" Before he could answer, she let out a little squeal. "Beach toys!"

"On a whim, I stopped at Sunsations."

Heather began pulling out the toys.

"I bought a bucket and shovel," he said. "And a beach ball—"

"We should blow it up."

"And a t-shirt that changes color in the sunlight."

"Oooo," she crooned, "Mia will *love* that."

"There are some other little doodads in here." He rested his hands on the back of one of the dining room chairs, watching Heather remove each item. "A dolphin necklace and ring set. A glass paperweight shaped like a starfish. And a pink rhinestone tiara."

"You found a tiara at Sunsations?"

He shook his head. "No. I bought that in Salisbury. Where I found the teddy." He ripped open cellophane wrapper covering the beach ball and began blowing it up. "I think she'll like everything," he said between breaths.

She peered into the now-empty bag, and then looked at him. "Wrapping paper?"

"I didn't think about that," he confessed. He forced a long breath into the ball's plastic nozzle. Then he paused long enough grin. "I didn't know we were going to have a party today."

"No worries. I have plenty of paper in the closet in my office. I'll run and get it. Tape and scissors too. Get that ball blown up! Be right back."

They spent the next half hour wrapping Mia's presents. Heather rolled the t-shirt into a cylinder, and by the time she'd finished, it looked a lot like a huge, brightly colored, ribbon-festooned Tootsie Roll. She laughed when she saw Daniel's attempt to cover the ball. And her comment that he'd used just as much tape as paper had him chuckling too.

Finally, the gifts were displayed around the cake, and while he lit the candles, Heather rounded the table to get her cell phone.

"Are you ready?" she asked. "You sing, I'll video."

"Got it." He leaned over the table, resting the

weight of his upper body on his splayed hands. His brow creased and he looked up at her. "Sing with me?"

His sudden bout of misgiving had her smiling.

"Of course."

As they sang the birthday song, Heather was careful to keep the phone as still as possible. She framed his face in a close-up shot, and slowly pulled back to reveal the cake and gifts. When the song ended, Daniel continued to look directly into the camera so Heather continued to let the video record.

"Mia, sweetie," he said, "I know you'll be home soon. I've missed you, honey. I can't tell you how much I've missed you. We're going to be together before you know it. I hope you're having a happy birthday."

His dark eyes went glassy with emotion.

"I wanted you to know that, even though we're not together, sweetie, I celebrated your birthday just like always. You might be thousands of miles away, but I can close my eyes and picture your face, and it feels like you're right with me. I think about you every moment of the day."

He lifted one hand and pressed it to his chest,

and Heather's sight went blurry as sudden tears welled.

"You're in my thoughts," he continued. "Constantly. Every day. You're in my heart. I love you, sweetie." The smile he offered took great effort. "I love you so very much."

Heather was mesmerized by the image on the small three inch by four inch screen. She watched him straighten, and the light from the birthday candles gleamed against the trail of tears that had slipped down his cheeks. He took a ragged breath and swiped his knuckle under each eye.

Seeing that he was no longer looking into the camera, she stopped the video. And only then did she realize that she too was crying. Her eye sockets burned, and the thick emotion that clotted in her wind pipe made it difficult to breathe.

He cleared his throat and took a slow, deep inhalation. The moment was so powerful, so raw. He missed his child, was worried sick about her, felt helpless over the whole ugly situation, and being apart from Mia on this special day magnified those feeling and tore him apart.

"Daniel, I'm sorry. This party was a bad idea." She shook her head slowly. "For some stupid reason, I thought it would be a happy thing. I should have realized you'd be upset. I'm very sorry that I've made you so sad."

She set the phone down on the table gingerly and rounded the table. If anyone on this earth needed a hug right now, it was him.

His hand rested on the top rail of the chair and he was turned slightly away from her. With his chin dipped low, it was clear that he was struggling to get himself under control. Heather wrapped her arms around him and rested the side of her face against the broad expanse of his back, and even though the action had been solely intended to offer him comfort, she'd be lying if she said she wasn't cognizant of deeper, more intimate, reactions stirring inside her.

His scent, warm and masculine, enveloped her like a cozy blanket, rousing to life a jittery feeling. Achy. Needful. Dangerous. Beneath her cheek, the knitted cotton of his sweater could not hide the rigidity of his trapezius muscle. Other parts of their bodies made contact, the small of his back and her stomach, their biceps, her hands on his chest. He felt so good, so solid, that all she wanted to do was surrender to her desire to sink further against him.

But before she could, he reached up and took her hands in his. In one deft move, he gently broke free of her embrace, turned to face her, and positioned her hands back around his waist. His fingers slowly trailed along her upper arms.

His touch left behind fiery, current-like tendrils that spread across her skin soft and velvety as liquid smoke.

He placed a sweet kiss on her forehead.

"Please don't apologize," he said. "I am upset. And I am sad. But this party was a great idea. When Mia has a chance to see the video, when she sees the cake, the gifts, the decorations, she'll know I was thinking about her on her birthday. And that will make her one very happy little girl. I have absolutely no doubt about that."

He dipped his head and placed a kiss on her lips. "Absolutely."

He kissed her again. "No."

Another kiss. "Doubt."

As he stared down into her face, he captured a lock of her long hair and positioned it over her shoulder.

The light, butterfly kisses made her smile.

"There," he said. "That's better."

The corners of his sexy, glistening lips curled up. Heather studied his face, the easy smile juxtaposed against dark eyelashes still damp with his tears, and something peculiar happened to her. She was overtaken by a fierce need to protect him.

From what, she wasn't quite sure. Physical harm. Emotional injury. Mental anguish.

Yes, that. All of that. She just didn't want him to hurt any longer.

"Mia will be home with you soon," she whispered. "I just know it."

His smile widened, painted with myriad emotions: hope, fear, despair, even shaky optimism.

"Of all the places I could have traveled to during this awful time in my life, of all the people I could have been with," he said, "I am so damned glad I've been here. With you."

A potent energy blazed in his eyes, and almost instinctively her chin began to lower. But he reached up, tucked his curled index finger beneath her jaw, and forced her gaze to reconnect with his.

"I want to kiss you, Heather. And I'm not talking about a little thank you kiss. I want to kiss you long, and hard."

He continued to stare down into her face, and her heart thudded like rapid cannon fire.

"I want to kiss you until you can barely breathe. Until I can barely breathe."

The words rushed at her, but his body remained utterly still. And Heather realized that, in his hesitation, he was asking her for permission. Now was her chance to say no. Now—right now—was the moment she should step out of this sensuous circle they had created.

But she lingered, motionless except for the rise and fall of her chest.

"I want to kiss you until you feel what I'm feeling."

He paused long enough to lick his lips, and watching his tongue drag along his dusky skin, Heather felt time slow to a crawl.

"Until the need raging through me rages through you. Until my heat sets your body on fire."

Curious sensations overwhelmed her; her heartbeat fluttered, yet her blood seemed to go thick and sluggish, excitement crackled across her skin like icy electricity even while heat beat like a drum at her very core.

"Heather?"

Realizing that his breathing was just as ragged as her own was what sent her over the limit of reason.

"Shut up and kiss me," she whispered.

His kisses were vehement, vigorous, and she gave as good as she got. She drove her fingers into his hair, pulling him tighter against her. Their breathing became panting, their desire very quickly turned to insatiable hunger.

He kicked off his shoes right there in the dining room, and she heard one of them hit the wall with a dull thud.

Moving almost as one, they kissed their way to the stair landing, fumbling blindly up the steps. She caught her heel on the header at the top of the staircase and she'd have fallen on her butt had he not grabbed her around the waist. They shared a burst of laughter that was both relieved and laced with frenzy, but the passion they had ignited quickly consumed them once again.

He tugged his sweater over his head and tossed it aside, and she slipped off her faux fur slippers. He pressed her up against the hallway wall, kissing her senseless, his hands planted against either side of her head, his body pressed against hers. She grew moist and need throbbed at the apex of her thighs.

The top-most buttons of his shirt came undone with ease, and then she fumbled beneath the shirt's hem and found his belt. He turned the door handle, and the two of them burst into the bedroom with enough force that the door slammed against the metal doorstop.

She *had* caught fire, just as he'd promised. She was frantic with wanting.

He stopped kissing her long enough to say, "It doesn't matter, Heather. I want you to know that."

Far off, she heard the sound of his zipper, the clinking of his metal belt buckle, as he removed his trousers. She bent and lifted her skirt, shimmying out of her panties.

They fell onto the bed and his lips were everywhere, on her temple, her cheek, her jaw, her neck. He stroked her arm with his fingers and she wondered at how such a light touch could wrest such a reaction in her. Blood whooshed through her ears bringing with it a light-headed, dizzy feeling she found exhilarating. And the feel of his body beneath her fingertips—the knotted muscles of his biceps and shoulders, the firmness of his belly and thighs—ramped up her exhilaration to sheer euphoria.

And still he continued to kiss her. His hot mouth moved slowly down the length of her neck and he nibbled his way along her collarbone. The open facing of his shirt dangled down as he hovered over her, the weight of the fabric brushing across her breast. She felt it through her top and her bra underneath, a sensation so rare that it felt nearly erotic.

She reached down and encircled the silky, cylindrical hardness of him, and she delighted in his raspy intake of breath.

With slow deliberation, he slid her full skirt up the length of her thighs. As the fabric swept across her skin, Heather held her breath, letting herself get lost in the passion emanating from his ebony gaze.

He touched her, the pads of his fingers grazing the soft mound of her curls and she closed her eyes, relishing each gentle caress, each seeking, exploring stroke.

"I'm serious," he said.

The rumble of his voice had her dragging her eyes open.

"The surgery. Your mastectomy. It doesn't

matter to me. Your... your reconstruction. And... and—"

His lips came together for a moment and a tiny frown creased his brow. The fog that enveloped her was too thick with yearning for her to take much note of it.

"Shhh." Sensing he wanted to say more, she reached up and pressed a quelling finger to his lips. "Not now, Daniel."

She shifted her hips, slid her legs further apart for him, and then gathering his shirtfront in her fist, she pulled him closer.

~*~

Heather's eyes fluttered open and she felt an instant of near panic as she realized she wasn't in her own room. But everything quickly came flooding back to her, and she smiled. Darkness cloaked the room in deep shadows; the glowing numbers on the digital clock read 1:12.

In the quiet, she listened to Daniel breathe, slow and rhythmic.

Her smile widened.

It wasn't as if she were a virgin; she'd made love

with a man before. But in so many ways this felt like the first time for her. Daniel had aroused a yearning in her that made her feel... well, as horny as a Texas lizard.

Humor bubbled up into her throat and she clamped her hand over her mouth to keep from chuckling.

She'd wanted him for so long; weeks of thinking and pondering and dreaming about what it might be like to touch him, kiss him, be touched by him. And now that they'd slept together, she realized just how paltry her imagination had been.

Nothing could compare to the taste of his mouth, the weight of his body on hers. Nothing would ever again make her feel so... womanly. So feminine. So desired. Yet falling asleep in his arms had been sheer paradise. Lying there in his embrace, surrounded by his scent, his warmth, had been absolute heaven on earth.

A twinge of discomfort forced her to move her shoulders, arch her back a bit, and she nearly gasped as the underwire in her bra speared painfully into the side of her breast. The elastic had shifted while she slept and it dug into her armpit. Finally fully aware of her physical state, she realized that the voluminous fabric of her skirt had become twisted so tightly around her waist that she felt like a lassoed cow at a rodeo.

She could hardly breathe. No wonder she'd woken up.

As carefully as possible, Heather sat up on the edge of the mattress. She waited just long enough so that she could make out the bed's footboard, the dresser, and the position of the desk chair, then she stealthily made her way toward the door.

Her feet bare, she padded across the chilly wood floor. She slipped into her room and softly closed the door. The one lamp she snapped on offered plenty of light for her to see how rumpled her outfit had become.

Heather tugged off her clothes, headed for her bathroom, and turned on the faucet in the shower. While she waited for the hot water to make its way through the pipes, she turned to face the mirror.

Why she would ever do such a thing was beyond her.

Mirrors were her enemy, the bearer of horrific images, the reminder of why she hated her body with such a passion, and over the years she had become deft at avoiding them. Especially when she was naked.

But now she found herself staring at her face, and her gaze slowly lowered.

Scars were curious things. In and of themselves, they were mostly harmless. A manifestation of the body's healing process. When skin was damaged—say, from a scalpel's blade—the body released collagen that resulted in a protective scab. Once the scab flaked off, a scar often formed. The extent of scar tissue was affected by many things, the size and location of the wound, ethnicity, heredity, even age.

Although Heather's scars had faded over the years, they remained pink and thick and slashed horizontally across the center of her breasts. But what sickened her the most was that which was no longer there. Where she used to have pretty, puckered nipples and areola the color of rosewood, she now had jagged, bubblegum-hued lacerations. In some areas, they were narrow as a thread, but the weight of her implants had caused the scars to grow wider in some spots. Thick as a flat, cotton shoestring.

She looked at her reflection and the only word that came to her was grotesque.

What man would look at the mess on her chest and find her desirable?

Daniel had whispered that her mastectomy didn't matter. But he had no idea what he was saying.

She couldn't imagine getting dressed in the same room with him. Or sharing the same bathroom. The humiliation of it would be unbearable.

Your mastectomy. It doesn't matter to me.

Had he been trying to set her mind at ease about their making love? If so, then why didn't he urge her to undress?

No, he was insinuating something deeper. Something longer-lasting than a mere one night stand.

She closed her eyes and tried to put together such a situation. How would it work?

How could she keep him from seeing her? Would she lock the bathroom door to shower? Would she scurry into the walk-in closet to get dressed every morning?

Is that how she'd want to live?

Total defeat filled the sigh that issued from her.

A waft of hot, stream-filled air rolled between her and the mirror, enveloping her in a foggy mist and obscuring her reflection from view. She turned wearily toward the shower.

CHAPTER ELEVEN

Heather held up the tiny newborn-size sleeper, inspecting it, front and back. The colors and decoration on the whisper-soft knit fabric was perfect—cute, yellow ducks sitting among sprigs of green grass. Sara wasn't far enough along in her pregnancy to learn if she was having a girl or a boy, so all the purchases made on this baby shopping spree were to be gender-neutral. Heather found a pair of white newborn booties too adorable to resist. Cathy had already made her purchase; a mobile for the crib fashioned out of large squares with black and white lines and circles as she'd read the vivid dark and light contrast provided good visual stimulation for newborns.

While Heather paid the cashier, Sara placed the basic, white cotton onesies on the counter next to the register.

"You two do not have to do this, you know," Sara repeated for what must have been the half-dozenth time.

"Are you kidding?" Cathy shifted the bag on her arm. "We're not picking out gifts for our precious bundle because we *have* to."

"She's right, Sara," Heather said. "Auntie Cathy and Auntie Heather intend to buy our way to being the baby's two favorite people in the whole world."

Cathy's eyebrows arched as she murmured, "And I spent the most today. Just saying."

Heather waved her off. "There's plenty of time for me outspend you today."

The three of them walked out into the parking lot, continuing to laugh and razz each other—because that's how their friendship had lasted so long, through a mutual free-for-all of heckling and mockery. It worked perfectly for them.

They'd met at the White Marlin Mall in West Ocean City a few hours before, each arriving in her own car, and they'd parked in what had become known to them over the years as "their" spot, centrally located in the lot so they could easily reach their favorite stores and remain close to all the restaurants.

After tucking her purchases into the trunk of Sara's car, Heather slammed shut the lid and turned to face her friends.

"You know, Sara," she said, "this bambino of yours is going to be my and Cath's only outlet for kid-spoiling."

"*What?* Why would you say that?" Cathy wagged her finger in the air. "I think you'd better just speak for yourself, missy."

Heather snickered. "I realize that getting married isn't a pre-requisite these days, but having viable eggs is."

Cathy's jaw dropped a fraction. "How dare you say my eggs aren't viable."

"I'm *saying*," Heather stressed, "that you're not

getting any younger, sweets. You'd better hurry your butt up."

"But I thought thirty-five was the new twenty-five," Cathy lamented.

Heather tossed her friend an ornery grin. "Cathy, at your next birthday party, aren't we going to play Musical Recliners?"

Humor got the better of Cathy and she chuckled. "And a game of Sag, You're It would be fun."

Heather snickered.

"Or, or," Cathy quipped, "Pin the Toupee on the Bald Guy."

"How about Spin the Bottle of Milk of Magnesia?"

"Okay, cut it out." Sara said. "Both of you still have plenty of time."

The comment surprised Heather enough to make her draw back. "Sara, I won't be having children. Ever."

Sara frowned, instinctively reaching down and placing her hand on the outside of her coat on her lower abdomen. Heather found the spontaneous action quite endearing.

"Don't say that." Sara placed her other hand on top of the one on her belly.

"I'm sure we've talked about this before," Heather told her. "I'm not taking a chance of passing on that horrible gene mutation to an innocent child." She shook her head. "Nope, no kids for me."

"That's sad, though," Sara said. "You'd make a great mom."

Heather shrugged one shoulder. "I'm just being practical."

Cathy slid her arm around Heather's, pulling her friend close. "You can spoil my kid when I have him. He's going to be cute as a freakin' button. You won't be able to resist buying him all sorts of crap he doesn't need."

Heather sighed. "Well, please don't wait until you're so old that going bra-less pulls all the wrinkles out of your face."

"I won't wait that long." Cathy grinned. "I promise."

"And we promise you that we won't let you go bare breasted. Ever." Sara offered an animated shiver, and then laughed as she tugged her scarf closer around her neck. "So what's for dinner? I'm starved."

Looking around at all their choices, Heather asked, "Sushi? Steaks? Pizza? What's it going to be?"

Sara's expression turned serious. "I think I have a sudden craving for pasta with pesto."

Cathy swept Heather along, hooking her free arm in Sara's and heading toward the Italian place. "The pregnant lady wins."

Heather happily told them, "Hey, I love warm, crusty bread as much as you do." Then she rolled her eyes and added, "Probably more."

The waitress had taken their salad plates and was clearing room on the table for their entrees. As soon as she left them alone, Sara heaved a sigh.

"Why do men have such a difficult time forgiving?" she asked.

"What do you mean?" Cathy tugged at the napkin in her lap. "You and Landon been fighting?"

Sara shook her head. "Oh, no. It's not us. But I suggested to him that he might invite his sister and her family to come to Ocean City for the wedding, and he's having a hard time coming to grips with the idea of getting over... you know, all of that."

The *all of that* that Sara was talking about was a great deal for anyone to get over. Landon's sister and her husband had gone against Landon's wishes and had sold the family farm back in Kansas right out from under Landon. His sister and brother-in-law had landed smartly on their feet after the sale while Landon had been left feeling as if he'd been hung out to dry. He'd gotten into his truck and driven east toward the Atlantic Ocean.

"Did you remind him," Cathy said, "that, without his Kansas trouble, the two of you might never have met?"

Sara answered the question with an uncertain smile.

The circumstances surrounding Landon and Sara's meeting had been so strange—eerily so, really—that the three friends were still uncomfortable talking about it.

"He'll come around, I'm sure," Heather finally said.

"He'd better hurry up." Sara leaned back to let the waitress set down the plate of angel hair pasta in front of her, and then she said a quick thank you before continuing the conversation. "I don't want to stand in front of the Justice of the Peace when I'm looking like a whale."

"Oh, stop. You're not going to look like a whale." Cathy picked up her fork and grinned. "A beach ball, maybe."

"Makes sense. Because that's what she's going to have," Heather chimed in. "Our little beach ball."

Sara just chuckled. She coiled a forkful of pasta and took a bite, savoring it with a long, drawn out, "Mmmmm."

"How's your mom?" Cathy asked Sara.

Geneva Hartford lived in Sara's house in the separate, downstairs unit. Years ago, the woman had suffered an accident that had damaged her back and she spent most days in some degree of pain.

Sara's face brightened. "I don't think I told you. Mom's doc is sending her to Philadelphia next month. I'm going to drive her up there. To a new spine center that recently opened."

Heather set down her fork. "Do you think they'll be able to help her? Is there a way to alleviate her pain?"

"Her doctor claims this place is cutting edge,"

Sara said. "He says great strides have been made in laser surgery for the back and spine. He seems to think, at the very least, they can treat her stenosis and make her more comfortable. He suggested it wasn't out of the realm of possibility that we might be able to do away with the wheelchair, and that she might be able to walk without a cane."

Cathy and Heather both ooo-ed over this wonderful prospect. No one deserved to live a life of misery, and that's exactly what Geneva had done since she fell down those stairs all those years ago.

Heather couldn't help but ask, "And how does she feel about all this?"

Sara twirled her fork in her pasta. "She refuses to let herself get excited. But I can see that she's... well, let's call it cautiously optimistic." She lifted the angel hair to her mouth but stopped short. "Cathy, she asked me about you last night."

"Oh?"

"One of the ladies from the church came to visit yesterday," Sara said. "She told Mom that she'd heard the Beach Patrol has come up with a new fundraiser for the spring. Mom wanted to know if you're planning to get involved since your Bradley is heading it up."

Cathy's exhale was audible. "He's not *my* Bradley. You did correct her, didn't you?"

Humor danced in Sara's eyes as she chewed and she lifted one shoulder in a slight shrug.

"Sar-*ahhh*," Cathy complained.

"Come on, Cath," Heather joined in the teasing. "Everyone in town knows he's your Bradley."

A cat-like arch raised Cathy's brows. "Oh, I think quite a few women in Ocean City think differently." Her mouth screwed up as she muttered, "Much differently." Then she shot a pointed look across the table. "Not that I mind."

Since her divorce, Cathy had always made it clear she'd never settle down again, and she'd never wavered on that conviction. Ever. Even during those times when she and Brad had those "on again" moments.

Heather couldn't resist a final poke. "Admit it. You mind. I mean, really, if you *were* to have a kid some day, I'd wager my B&B that the baby daddy would be Brad."

Cathy's smile waned and her face went red, and

Sara and Heather both immediately went into mollifying mode.

"Don't get your thong in a knot now," Sara said quickly.

"I was just teasing." Heather lifted her hands. "You know that." She murmured an apology, picked up her fork, and speared a delicate cheese ravioli. The sheet of pasta had been cooked to a perfect al dente and the filling was light and creamy.

"Did Geneva say what kind of fundraiser it will be?" Cathy asked.

Sara shook her head. "Only that your—" She stopped short by clamping her mouth shut, and she cast a contrite glance at Cathy. "Only that Bradley is heading it up."

"Well," Cathy muttered, "It's sure to be a success. I don't know how the man does it. He works part time with the Beach Patrol, part time with the EMTs, and volunteers more hours to more charities than any normal person could possibly spare. How does he make ends meet?"

What Heather heard was that Bradley worked jobs that mattered—he saved lives—as a lifeguard in the summer and a medical tech during the off season. And he volunteered a lot of his time which made him extremely philanthropic, in her view. Most people would be impressed with how he chose to live his life, yet Cathy made his endeavors sound... terribly lacking. How he paid his bills was his business. Heather suspected Cathy's attitude had a lot to do with Brad's womanizing ways, but wasn't going to risk ticking off her friend by saying it.

The physical nature of both his occupations forced him to stay in great physical condition, and with his blond, blue-eyed good looks, it was only natural that women gravitated to him, wasn't it? Why shouldn't he partake of the fun that came his way? Cathy made it clear, over and over, that she wasn't interested in him more than their occasional bed-buddy relationship.

Realizing that voicing these thoughts would only grate on Cathy, Heather didn't respond to what she knew was a rhetorical question.

"So how are things at The Loon?" Sara asked Heather.

Startled by the sudden change in the conversation, she just said, "Fine."

Cathy leaned toward her a bit. "Is the quiet still driving you nuts?"

The quiet? The house hadn't been so quiet last night.

A smile stole across her lips. "I'm learning to enjoy the quiet."

Cathy looked at Sara. "Is it me? Or is there something awfully cryptic about that answer."

Sara's mouth curled at the corners and she nodded. "Something's going on there, that's for sure."

"Something naughty?" Cathy asked Sara, then her gaze swept to Heather's face. "Are you bumping dirty bits with Daniel?"

Heather rolled her eyes and reached for her wine glass.

Using a low tone, Sara asked, "Are the two of you participating in genital gyrations?"

Heather nearly choked on the sip of wine she'd taken. She swallowed and coughed. "Sara! I expect that kind of vulgarity from Cathy, but not from you."

Sara's eyes glistened as she tilted her head and shrugged.

Sex between two consenting adults was normal.

Natural. Why should she feel embarrassed that her friends might discover that she and Daniel had slept together? Even as the question whispered through her mind, she could feel the heat creeping through her body, up her neck, and into her face.

"Oh. My." Cathy wiped her fingers on her napkin and then reached across the table to lightly smack Heather on the upper arm. "You go, girl."

The teasing humor that had shined in Sara's gaze a moment before now softened to pure delight. "I'm so happy for you, Heather. I mean it."

Self-consciousness continued to rattle Heather and she had a difficult time looking at them. She had no idea why. They were her friends, knew that physical intimacy wasn't easy for her, that inhibitions and fears kept her from being involved in a relationship with a man.

Certainly, her disquiet was caused by the indecision she felt about having had sex with Daniel. On the one hand, his passionate kisses and gentle touch had roused in her the most beautiful, freeing sensations she'd ever experienced; while on the other, having woken up with her clothing bunched and hiked and twisted around her like a noose had brought some stark revelations. How could something so wonderful also cause such wretched fear?

Easily, she thought, when her scarred, disfigured body was part of the equation.

Glancing up, she saw both of them staring at her, waiting in gleeful anticipation.

"I can't talk about it." The words came out sounding hoarse.

"Of course, you can," Cathy said with a chuckle.

"If you don't want to talk about it, Heather," Sara said softly, "you don't have to. It's okay."

"I have to admit, I'm... surprised." Cathy picked up her wine glass. "I'm... really surprised." Then she quickly added, "I'm happy for you, though."

"Really? Because if I remember correctly, you told me you didn't trust him."

Cathy didn't respond; she stared down into her wine, swirled the glass, took a drink.

After Heather's declaration that she couldn't talk about last night, she was surprised when the words began trickling from her mouth like a water from a leaky pipe.

"He was so gentle." Her gaze darted across the tabletop, settling on the salt shaker. "Yet he was so... urgent."

The food on her dinner plate was forgotten as she continued. "I told him about my operation. Not everything, mind you. Just about the mastectomy. Just enough so that he'd... understand. About my... body issues. And I do feel like he, well, like he got it, you know? He didn't try to remove my dress. Didn't try to open the zipper, the buttons. None of that."

Sara and Cathy had both gone quiet, and she knew they were listening intently to her.

"We were right in the throes,' she told them, "of these glorious..." She closed her eyes and inhaled deeply, remembering how it was to be with him. "What he made me feel was so amazing." Her words slowed. "So wondrously breathtaking."

She paused long enough to swallow and lick her lips, her eyes still focused on the small holes in the top of the salt shaker. "But in the middle of it all, he hesitated. He stared into my eyes and whispered, told me that it didn't matter. His assurance was so kind. What he said was, 'It doesn't matter. The surgery. The mastectomy. The reconstruction. It doesn't matter.' And the way he looked at me." She paused long enough that both Sara and Cathy went still. "It was as though... he had more he wanted to say." She shook her head, afraid she wasn't explaining her thoughts clearly. "I don't know. It was as if... he *knew*. Everything. As if he knew the truth about what my body looked like beneath my clothes."

Heather looked from Sara to Cathy, and the expression on Cathy's face made her do a double take.

"What is it?" Heather asked.

Cathy had gone as white as the table cloth. "I can't lie to you, Heather. As much as I want to, I just can't."

"What are you talking about?"

Cathy's throat convulsed in a nervous swallow. "He does know."

The three tiny words Cathy uttered sounded strangled and weak, but they were enough to stop Heather cold. She tipped up her chin and looked Cathy square in the face.

"*What?*" The question was ice-pick-sharp and out of her mouth before she saw the emotion welling in Cathy's eyes. A fat tear spilled, trailing down her cheek. Heather frowned. "I don't understand. What are you talking about, Cathy?"

Looking to her left, Heather saw from Sara's

innocent expression that she didn't know what was going on either.

"I'm sorry," Cathy whispered.

Confusion bit deeply into Heather's brow. "Sorry for what? What do you mean?"

"I didn't mean to." Cathy swiped at her nose with her napkin. "It was purely by accident, I swear to you. But I told him."

"Told him what?"

"I'm sorry, Heather."

"*Told him what?*" she pressed.

Cathy's usual cocksure attitude had vanished, and it was as if the fearful, apologetic woman sitting in her spot were a complete stranger.

"About the scars... and... and the rest of it."

Humiliation and shame rained down on Heather like a horrendous gale, lashing at her, stripping her bare.

He knew.

Her thoughts spun with such force, her head began to throb.

He knew.

Because Cathy told him.

Anger sparked to life like a lit match touching

dry kindling. The fire caught hold and burned inside her chest.

"How could you do that? Why would you tell him?"

"It was an accident. You have to believe me."

"An accident? How the hell could—" Heather yanked the napkin from her lap, tossed it onto the table, and stood up. "I am so out of here."

"Wait," Cathy pleaded. "You have to let me explain."

Sara reached out and grasped Heather's wrist. "Honey, sit down a minute."

But the fury blinded Heather. She shook Sara off and snatched up her purse. "I can't stay here. I can't look at your face another second, Cathy." The whole time she talked, she scrambled in her purse. Finally, she tossed money toward the center of the table and then grabbed her coat, not bothering to put it on before turning away from them.

"Heather, wait a minute! Come back. Please!"

"Shut up, Cathy," Heather called over her shoulder. She didn't give a single damn that people's heads were turning to stare at her, she just kept marching toward the door as she seethed and muttered through gritted teeth, "Just shut the hell up."

~*~

What made a friend?

The question tumbled across Heather's mind like grains of sand caught up in a stiff sea breeze.

Better yet, what made a *good* friend?

Someone who could appreciate the differences in others, came one silent answer.

She and Sara and Cathy all three had different personalities. They had different talents, different interests, but that never stopped them from loving each other and caring about one another. As different as they were, they also had shared interests. And over the years, they had focused on those, built on them, until they had forged strong friendships.

Good friends were open with each other, honest, and real. Heather knew down deep in her soul that Sara and Cathy were all of these things. Hell, wasn't it Cathy's particular brand of punch-in-the-gut honesty that had Heather sitting in her dark, freezing car, feeling so thoroughly infuriated that she couldn't—

No, it wasn't Cathy's honesty. It had been her utter betrayal that angered Heather. Never would she have imagined that Cathy would reveal her humiliating secret.

The mere thought had Heather clenching her fist and pressing her knuckles hard against her mouth and chin. Keeping her fury clamped inside was imperative. If she let go of her tight hold on her emotions, she knew she would scream and wail and pound the steering wheel.

It wasn't just rage she was containing. She was also filled with fear.

As she stared at the back door of The Loon, she realized that the temperature in the cab of her car had dropped to the point that she was beginning to tremble from the cold. Soon, she would either have go inside or she'd be forced to start the car and turn on the heater. Again.

Daniel knew.

He knew. About her scars. About her missing nipples.

That agonizing thought was worse than physical torture.

While he had made love with her, he had told her it didn't matter. At the time, she'd been blissfully ignorant of the secrets Cathy had revealed to him. And the fact that he had gone to bed with her while knowing the truth... Well, it was only logical that his reassurance had been sincere.

But he didn't *really* know. He had no clue just how deformed she looked. The contempt she felt when she looked in the mirror and saw the breasts of a mangled mannequin.

Her phone chirruped and seeing Daniel's name on the screen made her feel such dread that nausea began to churn in her stomach.

For the span of five long seconds, she considered letting the call go to voice mail. But he never called her on a whim. He must need something.

She slid her finger across the screen and lifted the phone to her ear.

"Daniel?"

"Heather, where are you?" Without waiting for an answer, he barreled ahead, "I've got to go. Mia's been found. Jakob is already on a plane with her. They're flying into JFK. I've packed my things. I'm leaving for New York. I had hoped to see you before I go. I've waited over two hours for you. I can't wait any longer. I have to go meet Mia."

Every vestige of dark emotion—anger, embarrassment, fear—evaporated like a puff of mist. She latched onto the joy she heard in his voice... and the urgency he was clearly feeling to be away, and all she could think about was seeing him before he left town. It was a strange shifting of emotion—craziness, really—but this kind of impassioned lunacy was something she was actually getting used to since meeting him.

"I'm here." She tugged the key from the ignition and then reached over to the passenger seat for her purse. "I'm right outside. I'll be there in five seconds. Five seconds!"

She struggled with the backdoor lock, making a mental note to squirt some graphite powder into it. After shouldering her way inside, she rushed into the kitchen. Daniel was standing by the table, an array of emotions displayed on his face.

Without thought, she set her purse on the counter, tugged off her gloves, tucked them into her pockets, and began unbuttoning her coat, but he wrapped his arms around her and pulled her tight against his chest.

"I'm so damned relieved, Heather," he whispered, pressing his cheek against her hair.

It was as if he were hanging onto her for dear life.

She slid her hands across his back, tucked her forehead into the crook of his neck, and closed her eyes. She couldn't begin to describe the rush of emotion that hit her like a tsunami. Sensations powerful enough to knock the breath out of her, bring her to her knees, whirled and eddied, filling her entire body.

The fact that he was sharing this precious moment with her brought her a stupefying sense of euphoria.

She loved this man, she realized in that instant. Loved him desperately.

"I talked to her, Heather."

"Mia? You did? I'm so glad." she asked. "Is she okay?"

He pulled away from her, but only enough so that he could look down into her face. "She's angry and upset. I didn't talk long because I... well, she started to cry when she heard my voice, and I couldn't make out what she was saying. Finally, Jakob took the phone from her, told me they had to go. Their plane was boarding."

Daniel shook his head, the memory making him frown.

"He didn't call me until they were changing planes in London."

"Why did he wait so long? It must have taken hours to get to the airport and fly to England."

"He was talking so fast. It was hard to catch everything he said."

Daniel ran his hands over her back and shoulders, and Heather sensed that he was taking comfort in touching her.

"Apparently, everything changed on Mia's birthday."

Heather tipped up her chin to look into his eyes. The smile curving his lips looked sad.

"My little girl knew I wouldn't let her birthday pass without planning something special just for the two of us. When she didn't hear from me, she became inconsolable. She screamed for me. Told anyone who would listen that she wanted to go home. She called Anica a liar. She tried to run away. Nothing Anica could do would calm her." His eyes glistened. "Mia wanted *me*, her daddy, and she was determined to get to me even if it meant going into double-time-tantrum mode."

"Because that's what she's been used to on her birthday," Heather breathed. "Being with you. Oh, Daniel, your making her birthday a father-daughter celebration over the years is what solved everything. It's what made all the difference."

She felt his shoulders lift a fraction beneath her hands.

"Isn't it crazy? Parents start family traditions and practices, we instill values, never knowing how our kids will be influenced by those habits and principles."

Heather let her fingertips glide down his arm a few inches. "Well, in this case the habit is what is bringing her back to you."

After a moment, he said, "Anica demanded to fly along with them as far as London."

Heather gasped. "And your father-in-law allowed that? *Why would he do that?* After what she did."

Daniel sighed. "She's his daughter, Heather. She'll always be his daughter. His only surviving daughter."

The last three words were spoken slowly and with gentle emphasis, as though he was forcing himself to come to terms with the situation just as much as he was explaining it to her. Heather might not like the notion of Anica continuing to be allowed access to Mia, but with that kind of clarification, at least she could understand Jakob's motives.

"He said Anica wanted to try to make Mia understand the meaning of family," Daniel continued. "But Mia would have nothing to do with her. She screamed every time Anica came near her. Finally, a flight attendant forced Anica to change her seat... for Mia's sake."

"Thank goodness someone was watching out for her."

"Jakob waited until Anica was on a flight back to Burgovnia before he called me. He knew I wouldn't want Anica anywhere near Mia. And he's right. I don't."

"That's understandable given what you've had to live through. Never feel you have to apologize for that. You're simply looking to protect your child."

"He's very worried he won't ever see his granddaughter again. He must have mentioned it a dozen times during the few minutes that we talked."

"How do you feel about that? About he and Anica spending time with Mia?"

"I honestly don't know." Daniel eased himself away from her, his hands lingering on her upper arms for a moment before he completely released her. "I can't even think about that right now. I just want to focus on getting to JFK. I've got a four and a half hour drive ahead of me." He glanced at his watch. "It'll be late when they arrive. Mia will be exhausted both physically and emotionally."

Heather hugged herself, the thought of his departure leaving her chilled and desolate inside.

"Do you know where you'll go?" she asked.

"A hotel near the airport for tonight. Then I'll take her home." His dark eyes latched onto hers. "But I'll be back."

Immediately, she lifted both hands, palms out. "Oh, I wasn't asking about that. I'd never press you about—"

"Shhh." He gently touched the pad of his index finger to her lips. "We'll talk. I promise. I have your number. I'll call you." His tone softened as he added, "And before long, I'll *see* you."

Heather nodded vaguely, then let her gaze slide

to the floor. There was so much she wanted to say, but there was no time in which to say it.

"I left a file folder for you," he said. "It's on your desk. I want you to wait to look at it... until you have a day when you're feeling positive. And open."

He went quiet, and when she saw his jaw clench, her brow knitted.

I want you to wait... until you're feeling positive. And open.

The words reverberated in her head, heavy and ominous.

Positive. And open.

"I don't understand."

"You will," he promised. "And we'll need to talk, I'm sure. I'll be happy to discuss everything with you." He reached for his coat and shoved his arms into it. "But I have to go now. I have to take care of Mia." He took a step to his left and lifted his suitcase from where it had been sitting on the floor.

Funny. She hadn't even noticed it there when she'd walked in.

"Of course," she murmured.

He closed the gap between them and bent to kiss

her cheek. "Thank you for everything, Heather." Sadness shadowed his small smile. "That sounds damned inadequate after all you've done for me. After all that's happened between us, but..."

He moved toward the door. "I'll call you."

She gave him a silent nod. "Good luck. Drive safe."

The latch on the door clicked, and the house was silent.

~*~

Hours later, Heather sat cross-legged on her bed, the half glass of wine sitting on the nightstand forgotten. The papers and photos from the file folder Daniel had left for her were scattered across the bedspread. She'd cried until there were no tears left.

He'd said that the awful results of her surgery didn't matter to him. But apparently they did. Why else would he have left all this... this... information? Pages and pages of research he'd done. The newest innovations in breast implants and implant surgery. Abdominal flap, gluteal flap, inner thigh flap procedures for skin extraction. New methods of tissue support, including synthetic mesh or something called acellular matrix. Nipple and areola reconstruction. Various tattooing techniques. Laser treatments for the lightening of scars.

Ever since her surgery, she'd felt repugnant. Deformed. She'd felt deficient, inadequate. And seeing all these grotesque images, this medical data, only served to confirm that Daniel felt the same way.

He hadn't actually laid eyes on her chest. What would he do, what demands would he make of her, if he *were* to ever see her disfigured breasts? Not that *that* would ever happen.

Her phone rang and she snatched it up.

"Yes?" She wasn't surprised that she hadn't been able to offer a proper greeting. There wasn't a single shred of pleasantry in her.

"Hey, I wanted to let you know I'd made it to JFK."

"Has Mia arrived?"

"Not yet. But she'll be here soon."

She could hear commotion in the background, people talking, a flight announcement being made. She had no idea what to say to him.

"Did I wake you?" he asked.

"No." Her eyes landed on the hideous photos lying on her bedspread. "Daniel, I don't want you to think about coming back here. You need to focus on Mia. Take care of your daughter."

He was quiet for a moment. "Heather, what's wrong? Why would you—?"

She heard his breathy exhale.

"You didn't wait, did you? You read the file."

"You shouldn't have gone to all this trouble." Her words sounded straight-jacket-tight even to her own ears.

"I didn't go to any trouble, Heather," he said. "That was all research I did for the book I wrote. I told you about it. I just printed it out from the file I already had on my laptop... in case you might find it helpful."

"Helpful?" She nearly choked on the word. "But I don't want more surgery. I had a terrible time with the reconstruction."

"Did you see the tattoos? The 3-D tattoos are amazing."

Heather hadn't thought there was any lament left in her, but her vision went glossy with moisture.

"You said it didn't matter." Her throat had closed to the point that the sentence came out sounding strangled.

"Oh, honey," he breathed. "It *doesn't* matter. Heather, sweetheart, it doesn't matter to me. I gave you the information because it matters to *you*. Every time I tried to kiss you, to touch you, you tensed up with... with... I don't even know what. I assumed it was fear. Of being vulnerable? Of being seen? I know you have a... a terrible apprehension about being in a relationship. About being left. About being abandoned. I felt it. Every time I came too close."

What he said was true. She'd spent a lot of years trying to get over the hurt Steve had caused her.

"I want you to be comfortable in your own skin," he continued. "I want you to look in the mirror and love what you see."

"I'll never love what the mirror shows me."

"*Like*, then," came his quick-silver reply. "I want you to be able to look at yourself and at least... smile."

She couldn't ever image that happening either. But his justification for giving her the file did make the tension in her throat and in her chest ease a little.

"But how do you know what I look like under my clothes doesn't matter to you?" she asked. "You've never seen me."

"That's very easy to answer."

The pleading quality left his voice, and his soft words sounded calm.

"Because I love you."

Heather's breath caught and held.

"I love your kindness, your caring. I love your beautiful face. I love your mind. I love your creativity. I have a wonderful video gift to show Mia. To let her know I didn't forget her birthday, and I have that because of you. I love your devotion—to your friends, to your home, your business. To me. You treated me with thoughtfulness and compassion. You were warmhearted when I needed it."

With each sentence he spoke, Heather's heart grew more tender.

"I love your laugh," he told her. "I love your wit. I love your body. I love the shape of your calves, the curve of your hips, the hollow of your cheek, the length of your neck. I love all of you, and that includes your breasts. I don't ever have to see them if you don't want me to. But if I ever do, I will love them... I promise you. Because they're a part of you, Heather. They're just one piece of the perfect picture that is you."

She didn't know what to say. His eloquent assertions had left her mute and wonderfully mystified.

"You're the kind of woman I want in my life."

Silence stretched over the air. Finally, he whispered, "Please talk to me, Heather. You're scaring me here."

"I... I don't really know what to say. I, um, I never expected anyone to say those kinds of things to me."

"I know you didn't. And I'm sorry about that. You deserve to be loved. Deeply. Thoroughly."

The sensual emphasis placed on the last word he spoke wasn't lost on her.

"Daniel, it scares the hell out of me to say this." She paused long enough to swallow. "But I love you too. So very much."

It was silly, really, but she could almost feel him smile through the phone.

"T-to tell you the truth," she told him, "after I

opened up the file and saw what was inside, I didn't expect to see you again."

His exhalation was filled with raw emotion.

"I suspected as much. Honey, that's why I left something behind. Something I need for you to take care of for me until I can get back to Ocean City. Back to you."

Heather clasped the phone tighter, straightened her legs, and scooted over to the edge of her mattress. The papers and photos crinkled, unheeded, beneath her.

"I left my laptop in my room," he said. "If you need to rent the room out before I can return, please put it somewhere safe, okay?"

His soft chuckle caused a cascade of chills to course across her skin. She was on her feet and moving toward his bedroom.

"You left your computer?"

The warm leather scent of him surrounded her when she stepped into his room. There it was on the desk in front of the window. His laptop.

She scooped it up in her free arm, pressed it to her chest, and sat down on his bed.

"But what about your book? Won't your publisher—"

"I have to focus on Mia right now. My little girl needs me. I have the rest of my life to write books. And I hope I'll do some of that writing while staring out at the Atlantic Ocean."

Joy swelled inside Heather until she thought she'd burst.

"Sweetheart, I have to go."

Sudden tension edged his voice.

"The plane is at the gate. I have to collect Mia. Deal with Jakob."

Heather nodded her understanding even though he couldn't see her, the phone call turned her into that much of an emotional wreck.

"It's going to be okay," she assured him. "Everything will be okay."

"We'll talk. Every day. I promise."

The call ended and she set the phone on the bed. She wrapped both arms around the flat, rectangular-shaped plastic and metal case filled with electronic components, hugging it tightly as if it were some sort of beloved effigy. For the moment, that's exactly what it was—a representation of the man she loved.

She leaned over, resting her head on his pillow

and tucking her feet up on the bed. She couldn't stop the beaming smile that spread across her lips.

He was coming back.

He loved her. And he was coming back. That's all that mattered. Everything else would be worked out in time.

Epilogue

Spring always arrived a little later along the coast than in those places located further inland. Although there were early-bird tourists already staying at The Loon who were right now splashing in the water and enjoying the sunshine on this glorious May day, the ocean temperatures were still the kind of chilly that left a person gasping if they were hit, unawares, by a frothy wave. Heather wouldn't venture into the sea to enjoy a swim for at least another month.

Pushing herself out of the porch rocker, she walked to the railing and glanced up the boardwalk. People strolled, others jogged, and a few rode past on bicycles, all of them with smiles on their faces as another tourist season began. Warmer weather and having people in the house after the last few cold, lonely months lifted Heather's spirits.

The winter nights seemed to drag after Daniel had left. He'd taken Mia home to his condo in New York with the idea of bringing her to visit Heather in Ocean City after a couple of weeks. But Mia had been so traumatized by her ordeal, that Daniel had sought the help of a therapist who had recommended intensive counseling along with getting the child back on her normal routine and staying on it for the foreseeable future—or until Mia felt safe again. So Daniel had heeded the advice, and he and Mia kept to the familiar. Mia had gone back to the private school where she felt safe, where she knew her classmates and her teacher. She spent her evenings and weekends with her daddy doing those things they enjoyed, playing in the snow, taking walks in the park, going to dance class and piano lessons, watching their favorite shows on television, and dozens of other ordinary activities, all in the hopes that Mia would understand that she was secure and no longer vulnerable.

Although Daniel's publisher told him to take the time he needed to get his daughter mentally and emotionally healthy, Heather had ended up shipping his laptop to him so he could write. She deeply appreciated the fact that he'd left it behind as a token promise to return.

Heather had heard all about his slow progress on the book, all about his and Mia's daily activities when she and Daniel had communicated either by phone calls, texts, or elaborate emails. Heather and Daniel had agreed that it was in Mia's best interest that Heather remain in the shadows. At least, for a while. The poor child needed this time with her father so she could put her frightful experience behind her.

After many weeks of working with the therapist, Mia had been deemed by her doctor as being ready to venture outside her safe coccon. So Daniel and his daughter were on their way to Ocean City and were due to arrive at any time.

Even though hundreds of miles had been between Heather and Daniel, she had never felt more loved. In a way, the distance had been a good thing, because their long phone conversations had allowed them to get to know one another thoroughly. For instance, she'd learned that his favorite meal was fish and chips, his favorite dessert was strawberry shortcake, while Mia liked pizza more than any other food in the world. Heather had discovered how much Daniel loved to shovel snow in winter, that Mia had decided her new favorite toy was the teddy her daddy had bought her for her birthday, and that Daniel had a lucky pair of orange socks he wore on days when he needed to write but the words wouldn't come.

Heather had realized over the weeks that she had a love hate relationship with that time near the end of their conversations when they said their goodbyes. She would begin to pine for him even before the line was severed, but her heart would soar when he signed off by telling her he loved her. His unexpected texts, which arrived at odd times of the day and night, had quickly become her absolute favorites. Romantic, profound, funny, his short messages never failed to put a smile on her face. She'd printed out the ones that made her heart melt down her ribs like gooey caramel over a hot flame, the ones that made her laugh, the ones that made her think. The habit might seem sophomoric, but she wasn't going to apologize to anyone for reading and then re-reading the words she found so alluring. She had even succeeded in memorizing some of them.

I want to hold you in my arms, breathe you in, set you on fire so you just might begin to know how I burn for you.

I'm lying here awake... can't sleep... amazed to realize that my—OUR—reality is so much better, so much brighter, than anything I could ever create for characters in a story.

Sometimes I miss you so much I think I'm going crazy. But that's because I'm so in love in with you. Do you feel crazy too?

No matter how far apart we are, you fill every nook and cranny of my mind.

I want to be the reason you look down at your phone and smile. Just don't walk into a fire hydrant. That would hurt.

251

When I'm missing you most, I close my eyes and imagine I'm kissing you... I wonder if you can taste it.

"Hey!"

Heather opened her eyes, squinting against the bright sunlight, and she swiveled her head to see Sara skipping up the steps.

"Hey, yourself," Heather greeted, rubbing away the goose-flesh that had risen on her arms while she'd been lost in thought.

Sara wore a loose-fitting blouse to cover the small baby-bump that was just beginning to show. "I haven't seen you for few days," Sara said as soon as she was on the porch.

Ever since Cathy's betrayal, Heather had become withdrawn. She tried not to let it affect her relationship with Sara; however, every time the two of them were together, there was an awkwardness that couldn't be denied. The "missing link" that was Cathy was extremely glaring.

"I've been busy with guests," Heather told her.

"Cathy says you haven't called her about the bridal shower. You are going to come, right?" Then she rushed to ask, "Oh, Heather, when are you going to forgive her? I miss you two."

Heather's answer was a mere whisper. "I don't know if I can."

"She didn't mean it. She swears it was an accident."

"Cathy doesn't do anything by accident."

Heather heard a tad of frustration in Sara's sigh.

"Look, I'm coming to your bridal shower," she assured Sara. "I plan on dancing at your wedding. I'll host your baby shower. I don't want you to think I would miss a single important celebration in your life... because I won't."

Although Sara smiled with gratitude, Heather knew her assurances didn't go as far as her friend would have liked. But there wasn't much Heather could do about that. Every time she thought about what Cathy had done, Heather's wounded feelings felt raw all over again. And if she thought about it too long, her anger would flare. So she tried hard to focus on other things.

"So today's the big day, huh?' Sara asked.

"Yes." The spring breeze caught a strand of Heather's hair and blew it across her face. "I'm so excited I don't know what to do with myself."

"Are you ready for them?"

Heather nodded. "I think so. Daniel said Mia can still be a little clingy at times, so I set up a roll-away in his room so she'll have her own bed but can still feel safe. I bought ingredients to make home-made pizzas for dinner tonight. It's her favorite, and I thought she might get a kick out of patting out the dough and adding the toppings herself."

"She's going to love that."

"I hope so," Heather murmured.

Sara snaked her arm around Heather's and gave her a quick, reassuring squeeze. "Come on, now. You and Mia are going to get along just fine."

The women stood, staring out at the beach for a few moments, then Sara said, "I haven't asked for a while... How are you feeling? All healed up?"

When Heather had first opened the folder of breast reconstruction research Daniel had left for her, she'd been dead-set against having any work done. But for several weeks she thought about little else. And the longer she looked at the images—of the women in the before and after photographs *and* at her own reflection in the mirror—she'd finally decided at the end of March to drive up to Baltimore for 3-D tattoos. Sara had agreed to go with her and the two of them had made a weekend of it.

"I'm good," she told Sara. "I was sore for a while. Red, inflamed. And the scabs were uncomfortable too. Dear Lord, I don't mind saying I'm glad the itching phase is over. I thought I would go nuts."

Sara winced at the thought, then she hesitantly asked, "Are you happy with the results?"

Heather looked into her friend's face, her slow smile growing until it beamed. "They're amazing. So beautiful, Sara. It's nothing short of a miracle. I'm just astounded every time I look at myself in the mirror."

"Oh, honey, that's wonderful."

"I never thought I'd hear myself say this..." She bit her bottom lip for a second before finishing, "But I can't wait for Daniel to see me naked."

Sara's head tilted, her shoulders rounded, and her eyes glistened with a mixture of elation and tenderness.

Emotion swarmed inside Heather and she looked away toward the boardwalk, fighting off tears.

And that's when she saw Daniel. Black curls hung over his ears and grazed his shirt collar, proof that he was in need of a haircut. The familiar angles of his jaw and cheekbones sent a thrill through her. She'd been so hungry for the sight of him.

He must have parked in the lot off the alley because he was opening the gate at the side of the property. Clearly, he wanted Mia's first glimpse of The Lonely Loon to be from the front.

The dark-haired little girl raced across the boards, straight to the sea wall, and Daniel lifted her up to stand on the wide expanse of cement. Heather watched father and daughter exchange conversation, heads bent together as Mia pointed first out toward the surf, then at the gulls flying high above in the clear, azure sky.

"They're here," Sara said. "I should go."

"No, please. Stay with me. It's fine. In fact, it would probably be best—"

"Heather." Sara clamped her hand over Heather's and held on. "Mia is going to love you. I mean it. Stop worrying."

Heather smiled her thanks. "Let's go meet them?"

Sara nodded, and the two of them started down the porch stairs.

Only a few yards away, Daniel turned to look at the B&B, saw them immediately, and lifted his hand in greeting. He spoke to Mia and helped her off the wall. The instant the child noticed Heather and Sara, she seemed to shrink a few inches in stature, automatically reaching for her daddy's hand.

"Hi," Daniel said when he and Mia reached them.

"I'm so glad to see you." It took every ounce of Heather's self-control not to reach out and hug him. "How was the drive? Was there much traffic?"

"It wasn't bad."

They stared at one another, and Heather smoldered inside as she realized he, too, wanted to reach out to her. She searched his gaze for only a second or two, just long enough for them to silently communicate the necessity for restraint and patience. There would be a time for them to greet each other in a proper fashion, a time they would be free to express the love—*the need*—smoldering inside them.

"Hi, Sara," Daniel said.

Sara didn't hesitate; she leaned and greeted Daniel with a hug. "You're looking good. I'm so glad you're back to visit us." When she stepped away from him, she looked down at Mia. "And who's this?" she asked brightly.

"Sara, this is my daughter, Mia." He looked down. "Mia, this is Sara. She runs the sweet shop right there. And this is Heather. She owns The Lonely Loon. The B&B I told you about, where we'll be staying this weekend."

"Such a pretty little girl," Sara cooed.

"Hi, Mia." Heather bent at the knees so she could look the little girl in the eyes.

Mia glanced shyly up at Daniel, then back at Heather. "You're the lady who made the video. You and daddy sang Happy Birthday to me."

Heather nodded. "That's me."

"Remember I told you," Daniel said to Mia, "that Heather baked your birthday cake?" Daniel chuckled. "Heather, Mia has watched that video at least a hundred times."

"It was a pretty cake," Mia told Heather.

Heather couldn't resist reaching out and touching one of the child's long, dark curls. "How would you like to make one this weekend?"

"With the sprinkles?" Mia breathed.

"I always keep sprinkles in the cupboard in my kitchen."

Mia's lips split into a smile, and Heather wondered if the sun had suddenly become brighter.

"Hey, Mia, I was wondering," Sara said, "if you might help me out in the shop? If it's okay with your dad, that is. You see, I made brownies today and I need to taste test them. You know, make sure they're sweet and chocolaty before I put them in the display case for customers."

"Brownies?" Mia's voice bubbled with a mixture of both awe and trepidation.

Heather stood, giving Sara center stage. She knew her friend was trying to buy her and Daniel a few minutes for a proper hello, and she was truly grateful.

"Yes." Sara bent forward and cupped her knees with her palms. "I have brownies with walnuts, and brownies with chocolate chips, and brownies with thick, glossy fudge frosting."

Mia's eyes grew rounder with each option mentioned. She looked up at her father, her fingers curling tighter around his, a question in her gaze.

"You can go if you like," Daniel told her gently.

"Remember, Dr. Barrett said it's okay. As long as you and I feel safe about what you want to do. And I do. Feel safe, I mean. I know Sara. But if you'd rather stay with me, that's fine. We'll go get our suitcases from the car and take them inside."

Long seconds ticked by, and Heather could see Mia contemplating her choices.

Finally, Daniel said, "Whatever you want to do is okay."

Mia looked a Sara. "I guess I could help you."

Sara beamed as she took Mia's hand. "I'll bring you right back as soon as we finish our taste test."

Heather watched them go into Sara's shop, and Daniel whispered in her ear, "Is there someplace we can go? If I don't get to kiss you right now, I'm going to lose my mind."

When the two of them turned to head up the steps to the B&B, they both caught sight of Cathy standing at the window of the cafe. She lifted a hand in greeting, and Daniel returned her wave. He didn't seem to notice that Heather didn't respond, he was that eager to get her alone. He took her hand and tugged her forward. Cathy held Heather's gaze for a moment longer before turning away.

Inside the cool, darkened foyer, Heather and Daniel wrapped their arms around each other.

"Oh, Heather, I've missed you so bad," he whispered.

And their mouths met, and clung. He kissed her until her heart was racing and her thoughts were spinning. And her body burned.

He groaned in frustration. "There's so much I want to do." He kissed her. "I wish we had longer than the weekend." He kissed her again. "But school will be out in a few short weeks, and we can come back for the summer. Mia and I have already talked about it. She'd love to spend the summer at the beach."

He pulled back, sudden doubt making his gaze widen. "Will you have room for us for the summer?"

"Are you kidding me?" She pressed her palms gently to his cheeks. "Of course, I have room. There will always be a place for you and Mia here. Always. I want you to think of this as your home."

Heather kissed him, digging her fingers into his thick hair.

"There's so much to think about," he whispered frantically. His hands trailed over her hips, settled on her waist. "I have a condo there, you have a house here. Heather, I just want to be with you."

Her quick kiss shut him up.

"We'll work it out," she told him, pleased by the absolute confidence she heard in her own voice. This man had changed her. His love had been transforming.

"I love you."

"I love you too."

Their long, slow kiss left them both in a fever.

"How long does it take to eat a brownie?" he asked, his breath warm and silky against her mouth.

Heather grinned at the desperation in his tone, delighted to know she was the cause.

"Sara will keep her busy. I have no doubt."

Their gazes caught and lit when the idea came to them simultaneously.

"We'll have to hurry," he said.

"Of course, we'll hurry."

Laughing like teenagers getting away with some seriously sensuous shenanigans, they clasped hands and raced for the stairs.

~ ~ ~

Thank you for taking the time to read Two

Hearts in Winter. If you enjoyed the book, please tell a friend about it or consider writing a review. Word-of-mouth recommendation is the best advertising tool an author can have!

A Note From The Author

I love the beach. So much so, that I moved to the seashore. You can see the sunrise pictures I post on Facebook, Instagram, Twitter, and other social media. Mountains and meadows, rocky cliffs and forests are all beautiful, but there is something calming about the ocean, something that calls to the deepest part of my being. I couldn't think of a better place to set The Ocean City Boardwalk Series than by the sea. I hope you enjoyed spending a little time in Ocean City, Maryland. I also hope you'll look for other books in the series: Book 1, FOLLOWING HIS HEART is Sara and Landon's story; I'll be writing Cathy and Bradley's story next.

The "family" that visited The Lonely Loon on

Christmas Eve (in Chapter One), including sweet little Izzie, is featured in AN ALMOST PERFECT CHRISTMAS. Although Christy and Aaron face tragedy, they also find a deep and abiding love. The book is available in paperback and as an eBook for Kindle, iBook, Nook, Kobo, and Google Play.

If you would like to make the International Holiday Dinner that Heather prepared for her Christmas party, please find the recipes on the following pages. Enjoy!

All my love,
Donna Fasano

Sweet Potato Soup (Africa)

Ingredients:

  1 tablespoon olive oil

  1 large onion, chopped

  2 cloves garlic, minced

  2 teaspoons ground ginger

  1 1/2 teaspoons ground cumin

  1 1/2 teaspoons ground coriander

  1/2 teaspoon ground cinnamon

  3 medium tomatoes, chopped

  1 1/2 pounds sweet potatoes, peeled, chopped

  1 carrot, peeled, chopped

  4 1/2 cups chicken broth (canned is fine)

  1 teaspoon salt

  1/2 teaspoon black pepper (optional)

  1/8 teaspoon cayenne pepper

  1/3 cup chopped, unsalted dry-roasted peanuts

2 tablespoons creamy peanut butter
1/2 cup fresh parsley, minced fine

Directions

1. Heat the olive oil in a large saucepan over medium-high heat. Sauté the onion until golden, about 8-10 min. Add the garlic, ginger, cumin, coriander, and cinnamon. Stir in the tomatoes, sweet potatoes, and carrot. Cook and stir for 5 minutes.

2. Pour the chicken broth into the saucepan. Add salt, black pepper, and cayenne pepper. Bring to a boil, reduce heat, and simmer until vegetables are tender, about 25-30 minutes.

3. Remove the soup mixture from heat. Using a food processor or blender, blend the soup and peanuts until almost smooth. Return to the saucepan. Whisk in the peanut butter, and cook on medium heat until just heated through. Serve warm topped with minced parsley.

Cornish Beef Pasties (England)

Ingredients:

For the pastry dough:

3 3/4 cups all-purpose flour (plus extra for dusting)

1 teaspoon salt

1/2 teaspoon black pepper

1 cup (2 sticks) cold butter, diced into 1/2 inch pieces

3/4 cup ice water (you might not need all of it)

Egg wash for the pasties:

1 large egg, beaten

1 tablespoon light cream

For the filling:

12 ounces steak (sirloin or strip), cubed into 1/2 inch pieces

2 cups onion, diced

2 cups red potatoes, cubed into 1/2 inch pieces

2 cups carrots, peeled, diced

1 teaspoon salt

1/2 teaspoon freshly ground pepper

3 tablespoons extra-virgin olive oil

1 teaspoon dried thyme

1 teaspoon dried rosemary

Directions:

1. Make the pastry dough: Place the flour, salt, and pepper in a food processor fitted with the 'S' blade and pulse them together just to combine. Add the butter and pulse at 1-second intervals until the largest pieces of butter are the size of chickpeas. Remove the lid, pour 1/2 cup of the ice water evenly over the flour mixture, replace the lid, and pulse a few times. Add just enough of the left over ice water so that the dough holds together when you press it between your fingers. Do not over mix as it will make the dough tough.

2. Place the dough on a piece of plastic wrap,

gently pat it into a large rectangle. Wrap it tightly in the plastic and refrigerate it while you make the filling. Dough can be made several hours ahead of time, or the day before, if desired. Refrigerate until ready to use.

3. Make the egg wash by beating together the egg and cream. Set aside.

4. Make filling: Heat the oven to 400°F. Combine the steak, onion, potatoes, and carrots in a large bowl. Sprinkle with the salt, pepper, olive oil, thyme, and rosemary and mix well so that all ingredients are well-coated. Set aside.

5. Assemble the pasties: Cut the pastry into 6 equal pieces and shape each piece into a flat disc. On a lightly floured surface, gently roll each piece of pastry into a 9-inch circle. If the dough sticks to the work surface or your rolling pin, sprinkle with a little flour.

6. Place about 1 cup of filling on each round, a little to one side so you can pull the other side of the pastry over to make a semi-circle. Compact the filling to remove air, brush the edges with the prepared egg wash, and then

seal the edges together. Use a fork to decoratively crimp the edge of the pasties.

7. Place the pasties on a heavy duty baking sheet lined with parchment paper, brush them all over with the egg wash, and bake until golden brown, about 40-45 minutes. Serve hot with mustard on the side. Leftover pasties will keep a few days in the refrigerator in an air-tight container.

Hummas (India)

Ingredients:

    2 15-ounce cans chickpeas, rinsed and drained
    2 tablespoons toasted sesame seeds, ground
    2 tablespoon extra virgin olive oil
    1/4 cup fresh lemon juice (about 1 large lemon)
    1 teaspoon salt
    2 cloves garlic, minced

Directions:

1. Process all ingredients in the bowl of a food processor fitted with an "S" blade until smooth and creamy. Place in bowl and sprinkle top with a few sesame seeds and a drizzle of olive oil. Serve with warm naan (Indian bread) or bread of your choice.

Tabbouleh Salad (Greece)

Ingredients:

- 1 cup bulghur wheat, also called cracked wheat
- 1 1/2 cups boiling water
- 1/4 cup fresh lemon juice, about 1 large lemon
- 1/4 cup extra virgin olive oil
- 2 teaspoon salt, or to taste
- 1/2 teaspoon black pepper, or to taste
- 1 cup fresh parsley, minced fine
- 1 cup unpeeled cucumber, chopped
- 2 cups cherry tomatoes, sliced in half
- 1/2 cup jarred black olives, drained, sliced in half

Directions:

1. Place bulghur into a large bowl. Cover with the boiling water, add lemon juice, olive oil,

and 1 teaspoon of salt. Stir, cover and set aside for 1 hour.

2. Once bulghur has absorbed the water, add the remaining teaspoon of salt, the black pepper, parsley, cucumber, tomatoes, and olives. Stir to combine. Cover and refrigerate for at least 2 hours so the flavors can develop. This recipe can be made a day ahead and kept in the refrigerator until needed.

Lemon Ricotta Pie (Italy)

Ingredients:

1 9-inch deep-dish pie shell, unbaked (store-bought works fine)

Filling Ingredients:

2 cups full-fat ricotta cheese

6 tablespoons heavy cream

2 large eggs

1/2 cup white sugar

3 teaspoon grated lemon zest

1/2 teaspoon cinnamon

1 teaspoon vanilla

1/4 teaspoon almond extract

3 tablespoon all purpose flour

1 1/4 cups amaretti cookies, crushed

Directions:

1. Place the pie shell into a 9-inch glass deep dish pie plate and flute the edges. Set aside.

2. Make the pie filling: In a large bowl, add the ricotta cheese, the heavy cream, eggs, sugar, lemon zest, cinnamon, vanilla, almond extract, and flour. Stir until well combined.

3. Sprinkle the crushed cookies evenly over the bottom of the pie shell. Gently spoon the ricotta filling over the crushed cookies and smooth evenly. Place the pie in the refrigerator for 20 minutes.

4. Preheat over 350° F. Place the pie on a baking sheet and bake until the filling is firm when giggled, about 1 hour and 15 minutes (could be a little less, so check pie at 1 hour). When filling is firm, turn off oven and leave pie in the oven with the door propped open a little. If pie is cooled too quickly the top will crack. Cool completely before slicing.

Maple Cookies (Canada)

Ingredients:
- 1 cup butter, softened
- 1 cups brown sugar, packed
- 1 large egg
- 1 cup real maple syrup
- 1 teaspoon vanilla
- 4 cups all purpose flour
- 2 teaspoon baking soda
- 1 teaspoon salt

Directions:

1. Preheat oven 350° F. In a large bowl, cream together the butter and brown sugar until light and fluffy. Add the egg, maple syrup and vanilla. Stir to combine.

2. In a second bowl, whisk together the flour, baking soda, and salt. Add the flour mixture to the creamed mixture and stir until combined.

3. Shape dough into 1 inch balls and place on baking sheets 2 inches apart. Flatten balls slightly. Bake until golden brown, about 8-10 minutes. Remove from sheets and cool on wire racks.

Other Books by Donna Fasano

Contact The Author

Blog:
donnafasano.blogspot.com
Facebook:
Facebook.com/DonnaFasanoAuthor
Twitter:
Twitter.com/DonnaFaz
Pinterest:
Pinterest.com/DonnaFaz
Instagram:
Instagram.com/Donna_Fasano
Sign up for Donna's newsletter:
http://madmimi.com/signups/110899/join